JENNY CARROLL'S

MISSING

Sanctuary

POCKET
BOOKS

This book is a work of fiction. Names, characters, places and incidents are products of the author's imagination or are used fictitiously. Any resemblance to actual events or locales or persons, living or dead, is entirely coincidental.

POCKET
BOOKS

First published in Great Britain in 2003 by Pocket Books

An imprint of Simon & Schuster UK Ltd
A Viacom Company
Africa House, 64-78 Kingsway, London WC2B 6AH

First published in 2002 by Pocket Pulse, an
imprint of Simon & Schuster, Inc. NY

POCKET BOOKS and colophon are registered
trademarks of Simon & Schuster

A CIP catalogue record for this book is
available from the British Library

ISBN 07434 50442

1 3 5 7 9 10 8 6 4 2

Printed and bound in Great Britain by Bookmarque Ltd, Croydon, Surrey

CHAPTER

1

This time when it started, I so totally wasn't expecting it.

You would think I'd have figured it out by now. I mean, after all this time. But apparently not. Apparently, in spite of everything, I am just as big an idiot as I ever was.

This time when it started, it wasn't with a phone call, or a letter in the mail. This time it was the doorbell. It rang right in the middle of Thanksgiving dinner.

This wasn't so unusual. I mean, lately, our doorbell? Yeah, it's been ringing a lot. That's because a couple of months ago, one of my parents' restaurants burned down, and our neighbors—we live in a pretty small town—wanted to show their sympathy for our loss by bringing over beef Stroganoff and the occasional persimmon pie.

Seriously. As if someone had died. People always bring over gifts of food when someone has died, because the grieving family isn't supposed to feel up to cooking, and would starve to death if friends and neighbors didn't come over all the time with lemon squares or whatever.

Like there was no such thing as Dominos.

Only in our case, it wasn't a person who had died. It was Mastriani's, an Establishment for Fine Dining—*the* choice for pre-prom dinner, or catering local weddings or bar mitzvahs— which got burned down thanks to some juvenile delinquents who'd wanted to show me just how much they didn't appreciate the way I was poking my nose into their business.

Yeah. It was my fault the family business got torched.

Never mind the fact that I'd been trying to stop a killer. Never mind that the folks this guy had been trying to kill weren't just, you know, strangers to me, but people I actually knew, who went to my school.

What was I supposed to do, just sit back and let him off my friends?

Whatever. The cops nailed the guy in the end. And it wasn't like Mastriani's wasn't insured, or that we don't own two other restaurants that didn't get incinerated.

I'm not saying it wasn't a terrible loss, or anything. Mastriani's was my dad's baby, not to mention the best restaurant in town. I'm just saying, you know, the persimmon pies weren't strictly necessary.

We were bummed and all, but it wasn't like we didn't feel like cooking. Not in *my* family. I mean, you grow up around a bunch of restaurants, you learn how to cook—among other things, like how to drain a steam table or make sure the perch is fresh and that the fish guy isn't trying to rip you off again. There was never a shortage of food in my house.

That Thanksgiving, in fact, the table was groaning with it. Food, I mean. There was barely room for our plates, there were so many serving dishes stacked with turkey, sweet potatoes, cranberry relish, two kinds of dressing, string beans, salad, rolls, scalloped potatoes, garlic mashed potatoes, glazed carrots, turnip puree, and creamed spinach in front of us.

And it wasn't like we were expected to take, you know, just a little bit of everything. No way. Not with my mom and dad around. It was like, if you didn't pile your plate sky-high with stuff, you were insulting them.

Which was a very big problem, you see, because I had a second Thanksgiving dinner to attend—something I hadn't exactly mentioned to them, on account of how I knew they wouldn't exactly be too thrilled about it. I was just trying to save a little room, you know?

Only maybe I should have said something. Because certain people at the table observed my apparent lack of appetite and felt obligated to comment upon it.

"What's wrong with Jessica?" my great-aunt Rose, who was down from Chicago for the holiday, wanted to know. "How come she's not eating? She sick?"

"No, Aunt Rose," I said, from between gritted teeth. "I am not sick. I'm just not that hungry right now."

"Not that hungry?" Great-aunt Rose looked at my mother. "Who's not hungry at Thanksgiving? Your mother and father slaved all day making this delicious meal. Now you eat up."

My mother broke off her conversation with Mr. Abramowitz to say, "She's eating, Rose."

"I'm eating, Aunt Rose," I said, sticking some sweet potato in my mouth to prove it. "See?"

"You know what the problem with her is," Great-aunt Rose said conspiratorially to Claire Lippman's mother, but in a voice still loud enough for the guys working down at the Stop and Shop on First Street to hear. "She's got one of those eating disorders. You know. That anorexia."

"Jessica doesn't have anorexia, Rose," my mom said, looking annoyed. "Douglas, pass the string beans to Ruth, will you?"

Douglas, who in the best of circumstances does not like to have attention drawn to him, quickly passed the string beans to my best friend Ruth, as if he thought he could ward off Great-aunt Rose's evil death glare by doing so.

"You know what they call that?" Great-aunt Rose asked Mrs. Lippman, in a chummy sort of way.

"I'm sorry, Mrs. Mastriani," Mrs. Lippman

said. I gathered from her slightly harassed tone that, in accepting my mother's invitation to Thanksgiving dinner, Mr. and Mrs. Lippman had not known what they were getting themselves into. Clearly, no warning had been issued about Great-aunt Rose. "I don't know what you mean."

"Denial," Great-aunt Rose said, snapping her fingers triumphantly. "I saw that on *Oprah.* I suppose you're just going to let Jessica pick at that dressing, Antonia, and not make her eat it, just like you let her get away with everything. Those disgraceful dungarees she goes around in, and that hair . . . and don't even get me started on that whole business last spring. You know, nice girls don't have armed federal officers following them around—"

Thankfully, at that moment, the doorbell rang. I threw my napkin down and got up so fast, I nearly knocked over my chair.

"I'll get it!" I yelled, then tore for the foyer.

Well, you would have run out of there, too. I mean, who wanted to hear that whole thing—about how I'd been struck by lightning and consequently developed the psychic power to find missing people; how I'd been more or less kidnapped by a less-than-savory arm of the government, who'd wanted me to come work for them; and how some friends of mine sort of had to blow up a few things in order to get me safely back home—again? I mean, hello, that subject is way tired, can we change it, please?

"Now, who could that be?" my mother wondered, as I rushed for the door. "Everyone we know is right here at this table."

This was pretty much true. Besides Great-aunt Rose and me and my mom and dad, there were my two older brothers, Douglas and Michael, Michael's new girlfriend (it still felt weird to call her that, since for years Mikey had only dreamed that Claire Lippman might one day glance in his direction, and now, flying in the face of societal convention, they were going together—the Beauty and the Geek), and her family, as well as my best friend Ruth Abramowitz and her twin brother Skip and their parents. In all, there were thirteen people gathered around our dining room table. It sure didn't seem to me like anyone was missing.

But when I got to the door, I found out someone was. Oh, not from our dinner table. But from someone else's.

It was dark outside—it gets dark early in November in Indiana—but the porch light was on. As I approached the front door, which was partly glass, I saw a large, African-American man standing there, looking out onto the street while he waited for someone to answer the bell.

I knew who he was right away. Like I said, our town is pretty small, and up until a few weeks ago, there hadn't been a single African American living in it. That had changed when the old Hoadley place across the street from our house was finally bought by Dr. Thompkins, a physician who'd taken a job as chief surgeon at our county hospital, relocating his family, which included a wife, son, and daughter, from Chicago.

I opened the door and said, "Hey, Dr. Thompkins."

He turned around and smiled. "Hello, Jessica. Er, I mean, hey." In Indiana, hey is what you say instead of hello. Dr. Thompkins, you could tell, was still trying to adjust to the lingo.

"Come on in," I said, moving out of the way so he could get out of the cold. It hadn't started to snow yet, but on the Weather Channel they'd said it was going to. Not enough snow was expected, however, for them to cancel school on Monday, much to my chagrin.

"Thanks, Jessica," Dr. Thompkins said, looking past me through the foyer, to where he could see everybody gathered in the dining room. "Oh, I'm sorry. I didn't mean to interrupt your meal."

"No biggie," I said. "Want some turkey? We have plenty."

"Oh, no. No, thank you," Dr. Thompkins said. "I just stopped by because I was hoping . . . well, it's sort of embarrassing, but I wanted to see if . . ."

Dr. Thompkins seemed pretty nervous. I assumed he needed to borrow something. Whenever anybody in the neighborhood needs to borrow something, particularly something cooking related, we are almost always their first stop. Because my parents are in the restaurant business, we pretty much have anything you could possibly need to cook with, and generally in giant bulk containers.

Since he was from a big city, and all, I guessed Dr. Thompkins wasn't aware that in a small town, it's perfectly acceptable to ask your neighbors if you can borrow something. There was actually a lot I suspected Dr. Thompkins didn't know about our town. For instance, I suspected that Dr. Thompkins wasn't aware that even though Indiana officially sided with the North during the Civil War, there were still some people—especially in the southern half of the state, where we live—who didn't think the Confederates were so bad.

That's why the day the Thompkinses' moving truck pulled up, my mom was over there with a big dish of manicotti, welcoming them to the neighborhood, before they'd even gotten out of the car, practically. Mrs. Abramowitz, who can't cook to save her life, brought over store-bought pastries in a big white box. And the Lippmans came over with a plate of Claire's famous chocolate-chip cookies. (Her secret? They're Tollhouse Break and Bake. All Claire does is grease the cookie pan. Seriously. I am privy to secrets like this, and many other much more interesting ones, now that Claire is my brother's girlfriend.)

Just about everybody in the neighborhood, and a lot of neighborhoods farther away, showed up to welcome the Thompkinses to our town the day they moved in. I bet, coming from Chicago and all, the Thompkinses must have thought we were a true bunch of freaks, knocking on their door all day long, and even several days after they'd gotten moved in, with brownies and eggplant parmigiana and Snickerdoodles and macaroni and cheese and Jell-O salad and homemade coffee cake.

But what the Thompkins didn't know—and what we were all too aware of—was that our town, like the United States a hundred and fifty years ago, had a line running through the middle of it, dividing it into two distinct parts. There was the part Lumbley Lane was on, which also held the courthouse square and most of the businesses, including the hospital and the mall and the high school and stuff. This part of the city housed what people in my school call the "Townies."

And then there was the rest of the county, outside the city limits, which consisted mostly of woods and cornfields, with the occasional trailer park and abandoned plastics factory thrown in for picturesque effect. Outside town, there were still patches of illiteracy, prejudice, and even, in the deepest backwoods, where my dad used to take us camping when we were little, moonshining. Kids at school called people who lived this far outside of town, and who had to be bused in for school, "Grits," as that is what many of them purportedly have for breakfast every morning. Grits are like oatmeal, only not as socially acceptable, and without raisins.

In my town, Grits are the ones who still sometimes drive around with Confederate flags hanging off their pickups and stuff. Grits are the ones who still say the N word sometimes, and not because they are quoting Chris Rock or Jennifer Lopez or whoever. Although I happen to know quite a few so-called Grits who would never call someone the N word, just like I happen to know, from personal experience, a few Townies who wouldn't hesitate to call a female like myself with very short hair and a tendency to be a little quick with my fists the D word, or my friend Ruth, who happens to be Jewish, the K word that rhymes with it.

So you can see why when we saw the Thompkinses moving in, some of us thought there might be trouble from other people.

But it had been almost a month, and so far, no incidents. So maybe everything was going to be all right.

That's what I thought then. Everything's different now, of course. Still, at the time, all I did was try to put Dr. Thompkins at ease as he stood there in our foyer. Hey, I didn't know. How could I possibly have known? I may be psychic, but I'm not *that* psychic.

"Hey, *mi casa es su casa*, Dr. Thompkins," I told him, which is probably about the lamest thing on earth there is to say, but whatever. I wasn't feeling real creative, thanks to Great-aunt Rose, who is a major brain drain. Also, I am taking French, not Spanish.

Dr. Thompkins smiled, but only just. Then he

uttered the words that made it feel like it had started to snow after all. Only all the snow was pouring down the back of my sweater.

"It's just that I was wondering," he said, "if you'd seen my son."

C H A P T E R

2

I backed up until my calves hit the stairs to the second floor. When they did, I had to sit down on the first landing, which was only about four steps up, because my knees didn't feel like they would hold me up anymore.

"I don't—" I said, through lips that seemed to have gone as cold as ice. "I don't do that anymore. Maybe nobody told you. But I don't do that anymore."

Dr. Thompkins looked down at me like I had said a dingo ate my baby, or something. He went, his face all perplexed, "I beg your pardon?"

Fortunately at that moment my dad came out of the dining room, his napkin still tucked into the waistband of his pants. My mom followed him, with Mike—Claire, as usual, attached to his hip—trailing behind her.

"Hey, Jerry," my dad said, to Dr. Thompkins, holding out his right hand. "How's it going?"

"Hello, Joe," Dr. Thompkins said. Then he corrected himself. "I mean, hey." He took my dad's hand and shook it. To my mom, he said, "How are you, Toni?"

"Fine, Jerry," my mom said. "And you?"

"Could be better," Dr. Thompkins said. "I'm really sorry to interrupt your meal. I was just wondering if any of you had seen my son, Nate. He went out a couple hours ago, saying he was just going to run to the store—Rowena ran out of whipped cream—but we haven't seen him since. I thought maybe he'd have stopped over here to visit with your boys, or maybe Jessica. . . ."

Over on the steps where I'd sank, I felt color start to return to my face. Sure, I was relieved—relieved that Dr. Thompkins hadn't been asking me to find his son. . . . He'd merely been asking if I'd seen him.

And I was also a little embarrassed. Because I could tell from the glances Dr. Thompkins kept throwing me that he thought I was a freak of the first order for my weird reaction to his simple question about his son. Well, and why not? He hadn't been around last summer, or even this fall. He didn't know I was the one the press had dubbed "Lightning Girl." He didn't know about my "special" gift.

But you could tell Mike, snickering behind his hand, had figured out what had happened. You know, what I thought Dr. Thompkins had been asking. And he considered the whole thing simply hilarious.

"No, we haven't seen Nate," my mom said, looking worried. She looks worried whenever she hears about any kid who has strayed away from the parental tether. That's because one of her own kids did that once, and when she'd finally found him again, it had been in a hospital emergency room.

"Oh," Dr. Thompkins said. You could tell he was way disappointed that we hadn't seen Nate. "Well, I figured it was worth a try. He probably stopped at the video arcade. . . ."

I didn't want to be the one to tell Dr. Thompkins that the video arcade was closed. Everything in our town was closed, on account of it being Thanksgiving, with the exception of the Stop and Shop, which never closed, even on Christmas.

But Claire apparently had no problem being the one to deliver the bad news.

"Oh, the arcade is closed, Dr. Thompkins," she said. "Everything's closed. Even the bowling alley. Even the movie theaters."

Dr. Thompkins looked super bummed when Claire said this. My mom even shot her a disapproving look. And in my mom's eyes, Claire Lippman can do no wrong, on account of, you know, liking my reject brother, even if it is partly because of Claire that Mike is currently attending the local community college instead of Harvard, where he was supposed to be going this year.

"Oh," Dr. Thompkins said. He managed a brave smile. "Well, I'm sure he's just run into some friends somewhere."

This was entirely possible. Nate Thompkins, a sophomore at Ernest Pyle High School, where I am a junior, hadn't had too much trouble fitting in, in spite of being the new kid—and the only African-American male—on the block. That's because handsome, athletic Nate had immediately tried out for and gotten onto the Ernie Pyle High football team. Never mind that Coach Albright had been desperate for any players, given that thanks to me, three of his best, including the quarterback, had recently taken up residency in the Indiana state men's penitentiary. Nate supposedly had real talent, and that had thrust him right into the "In Crowd" . . .

. . . unlike his older sister Tasha, a bookish senior, whom I'd spied hovering around the classroom where the yearbook committee meets every day after school. The *yearbook* committee, okay? And the girl was too shy to go in. I'd walked up to her and been like, "Look, I'll introduce you." She'd given me a smile like I'd offered to suck snake venom out of a bite on her shin.

I guess Nate's extrovertedness was not an inherited trait, since Tasha sure didn't have it.

"I'm sure he'll be home soon," Dr. Thompkins said, and, after apologizing again, he left.

"Oh, dear," my mom said, looking worried, as she closed the door. "I hope—"

But my dad broke in with, "Not now, Toni," in this warning voice.

"What?" Mike wanted to know.

"Never mind," my dad said. "Come on. We've still got four different kinds of pie to get through."

"You made *four* pies?" Claire, who, unlike me, was tall and willowy—and who must have had a hollow leg or something, because she ate more than practically any human being I knew— sounded pleased. "What kind?"

"Apple, pumpkin, pecan, and persimmon," my dad said, sounding equally pleased. Good cooks like people who appreciate their food.

No one, however, that I could tell, appreciated Great-aunt Rose.

"Joseph," she said, the minute we reappeared in the dining room. "Who was that colored man?"

It is really embarrassing having a relative like Great-aunt Rose. It isn't even like she is an alcoholic or anything so you can blame her bad behavior on outside forces. She is just plain mean. A couple of times I have considered hauling off and slugging her, but since she is about one hundred years old (okay, seventy-five, big diff) my parents would probably not take too kindly to this. On top of which I have really been trying to curtail my tendency toward violence, thanks to a lawsuit I got slapped with not too long ago for deviating a certain someone's septum.

Though I still think she deserved it.

"African-American, Rose," my mom said. "And he is our neighbor, Dr. Thompkins. Can I get anyone some more wine? Skip, more Coke?"

Skip is Ruth's twin brother. He is supposed to have a crush on me, but he always forgets about it when Claire Lippman is around. That's because all the boys—including my other brother, Douglas—love Claire. It is like she gives off a pheromone or something that girls like Ruth and I don't have. It is somewhat upsetting.

Not, of course, that I want Skip to like me. Because I don't even like Skip. I like someone else..

Someone who was expecting me for Thanksgiving dinner. Only the way things were going—

"What's wrong with saying colored?" Great-aunt Rose wanted to know. "He *is* colored, isn't he?"

"Can I get you a little more creamed spinach?" Mr. Abramowitz asked Great-aunt Rose. Being a lawyer, he is used to having to be nice to people he doesn't like.

"What'd Dr. Thompkins want?" Skip asked.

"Oh, nothing," my mother said, a little too brightly. "He was just wondering if any of us had seen Nate. Who'd like more mashed potatoes?"

"What's wrong with saying colored?" Great-aunt Rose was mad because no one was paying any attention to her. Though she probably would have changed her tune if I'd paid the kind of attention to her that I wanted to.

"I heard the only reason Dr. Thompkins took the chief surgeon job over at County Medical was because Nate was getting into trouble at their old school." Claire looked around the table as she dropped this little bombshell. Being an actress, Claire enjoys seeing what kind of reactions her little performances generate. Also, since she babysits for all the rich doctor types when she is not attending rehearsals, she knows all the gossip in town. "I heard Nate was in a *gang* up in Chicago."

"A gang!" Mrs. Lippman looked upset. "Oh, no! That nice boy?"

"Many a nice boy's fallen in with the wrong crowd," Mr. Abramowitz said mildly.

"But Nate Thompkins." Mrs. Lippman, who was big-time involved with the PTA, shook her head. "Why, he's always been so polite when I've seen him at the Stop and Shop."

"Nate may have been involved with some unsavory individuals back in Chicago," my dad said. "But everybody's entitled to a fresh new start. That's one of the ideals this country was founded on, anyway."

"He's probably out there right now," Great-aunt Rose said, with certain relish, "with his little gang friends, getting high on reefer cigarettes."

Mike, Douglas, and I all exchanged glances. It was always amusing to hear Great-aunt Rose use the word "reefer."

My mom apparently didn't find it very amusing, though, since she said, in a stern voice, "Don't be ridiculous, Rose. There are no drugs here. I mean, not in this town."

I didn't think it would be politic to point out to my mom that the weekend before, at the *Hello Dolly* cast party (Claire, of course, had gotten the part of Dolly), two kids (not Claire, obviously— she doesn't do drugs, as an actress's body, she informed me, is her temple) had been hauled out by EMTs after imbibing in a little too much Ecstasy. It is better in the long run that my mom be shielded from these things.

"Can I be excused?" I asked, instead. "I have to run over to Joanne's house and get those trig notes I was telling you about."

"*May* I be excused," my mom said. "And no, you may not. It's Thanksgiving, Jessica. You have three whole days off. You can pick up the notes tomorrow."

"You know somebody graffitied the overpass last week," Mrs. Lippman informed everyone. "You can't even tell what it says. I never thought of it before now, but supposing it's one of those . . . what do they call them, again? I saw it on *Sixty Minutes*. Oh, yes. A gang tag. I mean, I'm sure it's not. But what if it is?"

"I can't get the notes tomorrow," I said. "Joanne's going to her grandma's tomorrow. Tonight's the only time I can get them."

"Hush," my mom said.

"Reefer today," Great-aunt Rose said, shaking her head. "Heroin tomorrow."

"You don't know anybody named Joanne," Douglas leaned over to whisper in my ear.

"Mom," I said, ignoring Douglas. Which was kind of mean, on account of it had taken a lot for him even to come down to dinner at all. Douglas is not what you'd call the most sociable guy. In fact, antisocial is more the word for it, really. But he's gotten a little better since he started a job at a local comic book store. Well, better for him, anyway.

"Come on, Mom," I said. "I'll be back in less than an hour." This was a total lie, but I was hoping that she'd be so busy with her guests and everything, she wouldn't even notice I wasn't home yet.

"Jessica," my dad said, signaling for me to help him start gathering people's plates. "You'll miss pie."

"Save a piece of each for me," I said, reaching out to grab the plates nearest me, then following him into the kitchen. "Please?"

My dad, after rolling his eyes at me a little, finally tilted his head toward the driveway. So I knew it was okay.

"Take Ruth with you," my dad said, as I was pulling my coat down from its hook by the garage door.

"Aw, Dad," I said.

"You have a learner's permit," my dad said. "Not a license. You may not get behind the wheel without a licensed driver in the passenger seat."

"Dad." I thought my head was going to

explode. "It's Thanksgiving. There is no one out on the streets. Even the cops are at home."

"It's supposed to snow," he said.

"The forecast said tomorrow, not tonight." I tried to look my most dependable. "I will call you as soon as I get there, and then again, right before I leave. I swear."

"Well, Joe." Mr. Lippman walked into the kitchen. "May I extend my compliments to the chef? That was the best Thanksgiving dinner I've had in ages."

My dad looked pleased. "Really, Burt? Well, thank you. Thank you so much."

"Dad," I said, standing by the heart-shaped key peg by the garage door.

My dad barely looked at me. "Take your mother's car," he said to me. Then, to Mr. Lippman, he went, "You didn't think the mashed potatoes were a little too garlicky?"

Victorious, I snatched my mom's car keys—on a Girl Scout whistle key chain, in case she got attacked in the parking lot at Wal-Mart; no one had ever gotten attacked there before, but you never knew. Besides, everybody had gotten paranoid since Mastriani's burnt down, even though they'd caught the perps—and I bolted.

Free at last, I thought, as I climbed behind the wheel of her Volkswagen Rabbit. *Free at last. Thank God almighty, I am free at last.*

Which is an actual historical quote from a famous person, and probably didn't really apply to the current situation. But believe me, if you'd been cooped up all evening with Great-aunt Rose, you'd have thought it, too.

About the license thing. Yeah, that was kind of funny, actually. I was virtually the only junior at Ernie Pyle High who didn't have a driver's license. It wasn't because I wasn't old enough, either. I just couldn't seem to pass the exam. And not because I can't drive. It's just this whole, you know, speed limit thing. Something happens to me when I get behind the wheel of a car. I don't know what it is. I just need—I mean really *need*—to go fast. It must be like a hormonal thing, like Mike and Claire Lippman, because I fully can't help it.

So really, my parents have no business letting me use the car. I mean, if I got into a wreck, no way was their insurance going to cover the damages.

But the thing was, I wasn't going to get into a wreck. Because except for the lead foot thing, I'm a good driver. A *really* good driver.

Too bad I suck at pretty much everything else.

My mother's car is a Rabbit. It doesn't have nearly the power of my dad's Volvo, but it's got punch. Plus, with me being so short, it's a little easier to maneuver. I backed out of the driveway—piece of cake, even in the dark—and pulled out onto empty Lumbley Lane. Across the street, all the lights in the Hoadley place—I mean, the Thompkins place—were blazing. I looked up, at the windows directly across the street from my bedroom dormers. Those, I knew, from having seen her in them, were Tasha Thompkins's bed-room windows. The Thompkinses, who had grandparents visiting—I knew because they'd turned down my mom and dad's invitation to Thanksgiving dinner on account of their already having their own guests—had eaten earlier than we had, if Nate had been sent out two hours ago for whipped cream. Tasha, I could see, was upstairs in her room already. I wondered what she was doing. I hoped not homework. But Tasha sort of seemed like the homework-after-Thanksgiving-dinner kind of girl.

Unlike me. I was the sneak-out-to-meet-her-boyfriend-after-Thanksgiving-dinner kind of girl.

And at that moment, I was more glad than I'd been in a long, long time to be me. I didn't won-der, not even for a second, what it might be like to be Tasha, much less her brother Nate.

Except of course if I had—if I had bothered to think, even for a minute, about Nate Thompkins—he'd probably still be alive today.

CHAPTER

3

"Gosh, Mrs. Wilkins," I said. "That was the best pumpkin pie I ever had."

Rob's mom brightened. "You really think so, Jess?"

"Yes, ma'am," I said, meaning it. "Better than my dad's, even."

"Well, I doubt that," Mrs. Wilkins said with a laugh. She looked pretty in the soft light over the kitchen sink, with all her red hair piled up on top of her head. She had on a nice dress, too, a silk one in jade green. She didn't look like a mom. She looked like she was somebody's girlfriend. Which she was, in fact. She was this guy Gary-No-Really-Just-Call-Me-Gary's girlfriend.

But she was also my boyfriend Rob's mom.

"Isn't your dad a gourmet cook?" Just-Call-Me-Gary asked, as he helped bring in the dishes from the Wilkinses' dining room table.

"Well," I said. "I don't know about gourmet. But he's a good cook. Still, his pumpkin pie can't hold a candle to yours, Mrs. Wilkins."

"Go on," Mrs. Wilkins said, flushing with pleasure. "Me? Better than a gourmet cook? I don't think so."

"Sure is good enough for me," Gary said, and he put his arms around her waist, and sort of danced her around the kitchen.

I noticed Rob, watching from the kitchen door, kind of grimace, then turn around and walk away. Maybe Rob had a right to be disgusted. He worked with Just-Call-Me-Gary at his uncle's auto repair shop. It was through Rob that Mrs. Wilkins had met Just-Call-Me-Gary in the first place.

After watching Gary and Rob's mom dance for a few seconds more—they actually looked pretty good together, since he was all lean and tall and good looking in a cowboy sort of way, and she was all pretty and plump in a dance hall girl kind of way—I followed Rob out into the living room, where he'd switched on the TV, and was watching football.

And Rob is not a huge sports fan. Like me, he prefers bikes.

Motorbikes, that is.

"Hey," I said, flopping down onto the couch next to him. "Why so glum, chum?"

Which was a toolish thing to say, I know, but when confronted with six feet of hot, freshly showered male in softly faded denim, it is hard for a girl like me to think straight.

"Nothing." Rob, normally fairly uncommu-
nicative, at least where his deepest emotions
were concerned—like, for instance, the ones he
felt for me—aimed the remote and changed the
channel.

"Is it Gary?" I asked. "I thought you liked
him."

"He's all right," Rob said. *Click. Click. Click.* He
was going through channels like Claire Lippman,
a champion tanner, went through bottles of sun-
screen.

"Then what's the matter?"

"Nothing," Rob said. "I told you."

"Oh."

I couldn't help feeling a little disappointed. It
wasn't like I'd expected him to propose to me or
anything, but I had sort of thought, when he'd
invited me to have Thanksgiving dinner with
him and his mom, that Rob and I were making
some headway, you know, in the relationship
department. I thought maybe he was finally
going to put aside this ridiculous prejudice he
has against me, on account of my being sixteen
and him being eighteen and on probation for
some crime the nature of which he has yet to
reveal to me.

Instead, the whole thing seemed to have been
cooked up by his mom. Not just the dinner, but
the invitation, as well.

"We just don't see enough of you," Mrs.
Wilkins had said, when I'd come through the
door bearing flowers. (Stop and Shop, but what

she didn't know wouldn't hurt her. Besides, they were pretty nice, and had cost me ten whole dollars.) "Do we, Rob?"

Rob had only glared at me. "You could have called," he said. "I'd have come and picked you up."

"Why should you have gone to all that trouble?" I'd asked, airily. "My mom was fine with me taking the car."

"Mastriani, I think you're forgetting something."

"What?"

"You don't have a license."

For a guy I'd met in detention, you would think Rob would be a lot more open-minded. But he is surprisingly old-fashioned on a large number of topics.

Such as, I was finding out, his mom and her dating habits.

"It's just," he said, when sounds of playful splashing started coming from the kitchen, "she has to work tomorrow, that's all. I mean, the whole reason we stayed here instead of going to Evansville with my uncle is that she has to work tomorrow."

"Oh," I said. What else could I say?

"I just hope he isn't planning on staying late," Rob said. *Click. Click. Click.* "Mom's got the breakfast shift."

I knew all about Mrs. Wilkins and her breakfast shift. Before it burned down, Rob's mom had worked at Mastriani's. Since it got toasted, she's been working instead at Joe's, my mom and dad's other restaurant.

"I'm sure he's going to leave soon," I said encouragingly, even though it wasn't even ten o'clock. Rob was way overreacting. "Hey, why don't we volunteer to do the dishes, so they can, you know, visit?"

Rob made a face, but since he is basically a guy who would do anything for his mom, on account of his dad having left them both a long time ago, he stood up.

But when we got into the kitchen, it was clear from the amount of suds being flung about that Just-Call-Me-Gary and Mrs. Wilkins were having a pretty good time doing the dishes themselves.

"Mom," Rob said, trying, I could tell, not to get mad. "Isn't that your good dress?"

"Oh." Mrs. Wilkins looked down at herself. "Yes, it is. Where is my apron? Oh, I left it in my bedroom. . . ."

"I'll get it," I volunteered, because I am nosey and I wanted to see what Mrs. Wilkins's bedroom looked like.

"Oh, aren't you sweet?" Mrs. Wilkins said. And then she aimed the dish nozzle at Just-Call-Me-Gary and got him right in the chest with a stream of hot water.

Rob looked nauseated.

Mrs. Wilkins's bedroom was on the second floor of the tiny little farmhouse she and Rob lived in. Her room was a lot like her, pink and cream and pretty. She had some baby pictures of

Rob on the wall that I admired for a few seconds, after I'd found her apron on the bed. That, I thought to myself, is how my kid with Rob would look. If we ever had kids. Which would have to wait until I had a career, first. Oh, and for Rob to propose. Or take me out on a real date.

In one of the photos, Rob, who was still young enough to be in diapers, was being held by a man whom I didn't recognize. He didn't look like any of Rob's uncles, who, like Rob's mom, were all redheaded. In fact, this man looked more like Rob, with the same dark hair and smokey gray eyes.

This, I decided, had to be Rob's dad. Rob never wanted to talk about his dad, I guess because he was still mad at him for walking out on Rob and his mom. Still, I could see why Rob's mom would have gone for the guy. He was something of a hottie.

Back downstairs, I handed Mrs. Wilkins her apron. She was still giggling over something Just-Call-Me-Gary had said. Just-Call-Me-Gary looked pretty happy, too. In fact the only person who didn't look very happy was Rob.

Mrs. Wilkins must have noticed, since she went, "Rob, why don't you show Jessica the progress you've made on your bike?"

I perked up at this. Rob kept the bike he was currently working on, a totally choice but ancient Harley, in the barn. This was practically an invitation from Rob's mom to go and make out with her son. I could not believe my good fortune.

But once we got into the barn, Rob didn't look very inclined to make out. Not that he ever does. He is unfortunately very good at resisting his carnal urges. In fact, I would almost say that he doesn't have any carnal urges, except that every once in a while, and all too rarely for my tastes, I am able to wear him down with my charm and cherry Chap Stick.

Or maybe he just gets so sick of me talking all the time that he kisses me in order to shut me up. Who knows?

In any case, he didn't seem particularly inclined to take advantage of my vulnerable femininity there in the barn. Maybe I should have worn a skirt, or something.

"Is this just because I drove out here?" I asked, as I watched him tinker around with the bike.

Rob, looking up at the bike, which rested on a worktable in the middle of the barn, tightened something with a wrench. "What are you talking about?"

"This," I said. "I mean, if I'd known you were going to be so crabby about it, I'd have called you to come pick me up, I swear."

"No, you wouldn't have," Rob said, doing something with the wrench that made the muscles in his upper arms bunch up beneath the gray sweater he wore. Which was way more entertaining than watching sports on TV, let me tell you.

"What are you talking about? I just said—"

"You didn't even tell your parents you were coming here, Mastriani," Rob said. "So cut the crap."

"What do you mean?" I tried to sound offended, even though of course he was telling the truth. "They know where I am."

Rob put down the wrench, folded his arms across his chest, leaned his butt against the work-table, and said, "Then why, when you called to tell them you got here, did you say you were at somebody Joanne's?"

Damn! I hadn't realized he'd been in the room when I'd made that call.

"Look, Mastriani," he said. "You know I've had my doubts from the start about this—you and me, I mean. And not just because I've graduated and you're still in the eleventh grade—not to mention the whole jailbait factor. But let's be real. You and I come from different worlds."

"That," I said, "is so not—"

"Well, different sides of the tracks, then."

"Just because I'm a Townie," I said, "and you're a—"

He held up a single hand. "Look, Mastriani. Let's face it. This isn't going to work."

I've been working really hard on my anger management issues lately. Except for that whole thing with the football players—and Karen Sue Hankey— I hadn't beat up a single person or served a day of detention the whole semester. Mr. Goodhart, my guidance counselor, said he was really proud of my progress, and was thinking about canceling my mandatory weekly meetings with him.

But when Rob held up his hand like that, and said that this, meaning us, wasn't going to work, it was about all I could do to keep from grabbing that hand and twisting Rob's arm behind his back until he said uncle. All that kept me from doing it, really, was that I have found that boys don't really like it when you do things like this to them, and I wanted Rob to like me. To more than like me.

So instead of twisting his arm behind his back, I put my hands on my hips, cocked my head, and went, "Does this have something to do with that Gary dude?"

Rob unfolded his arms and turned back to his bike. "No," he said. "This is between you and me, Mastriani."

"Because I noticed you don't seem to like him very much."

"You're sixteen years old," Rob said, to the bike. "*Sixteen!*"

"I mean, I guess I could understand why you don't like him. It must be weird to see your mom with some guy other than your dad. But that doesn't mean it's okay to take it out on me."

"Jess." It always meant trouble when Rob called me by my first name. "You've got to see that this can't go anywhere. I'm on probation, okay? I can't get caught hanging out with some *kid*—"

The kid part stung, but I graciously chose to ignore it, observing that Rob, in the words of Great-aunt Rose's hero, Oprah, was in some psychic pain.

"What I hear you saying," I said, talking the

way Mr. Goodhart had advised me to talk when I was in a situation that might turn adversarial, "is that you don't want to see me anymore because you feel that our age and socioeconomic differences are too great—"

"Don't even tell me that you don't agree," Rob interrupted, in a warning tone. "Otherwise, why haven't you told your parents about me? Huh? Why am I this dark secret in your life? If you were so sure that we have something that could work, you'd have introduced me to them by now."

"What I am saying to you in response," I went on, as if he hadn't spoken, "is that I believe you are pushing me away because your father pushed you away, and you can't stand to be hurt that way again."

Rob looked at me over his shoulder. His smokey gray eyes, in the light from the single bulb hanging from the wooden beam overhead, were shadowed.

"You're nuts," was all he said. But he really seemed to mean it sincerely.

"Rob," I said, taking a step toward him. "I just want you to know, I am not like your dad. I will never leave you."

"Because you're a freaking psycho," Rob said.

"No," I said. "That's not why. It's because I lo—"

"Don't!" he said, thrusting the rag out at me like it was a weapon. There was a look of naked panic on his face. "Don't say it! Mastriani, I am warning you—"

"—ve you."

"I *told* you"—He wadded the rag up and threw it viciously into a far corner of the barn—"not to say it."

"I'm sorry," I said, gravely. "But I am afraid my unbridled passion was simply too great to hold in check a moment longer."

A second later it appeared that in actuality Rob was the one suffering from the unbridled passion, not me. At least if the way he grabbed me by the shoulders, dragged me toward him, and started kissing me was any indication.

While it was, of course, highly gratifying to be kissed by a young man who was clearly so incapable of controlling his tremendous ardor for me, it has to be remembered that we were kissing in a barn, which at the end of November is not the warmest place to be at night. Furthermore, it wasn't like there were any comfy couches or beds nearby for him to throw me down on or anything. I suppose we could have done it in the hay, but

a) eew, *and*

b) *my passion for Rob is not* that *unbridled.*

I mean, sex is a big enough step in any relationship without doing it in an old barn. Um, no thank you. I am willing to wait until the moment is right—such as prom night. In the unlikely event I am ever invited to prom. Which, considering that my boyfriend is already a high school graduate, seems unlikely. Unless of course *I* invite *him.*

But again, *eew.*

"I think I should go home now," I said, the next time we both came up for air.

"That," Rob said, resting his forehead against mine and breathing hard, "would probably be a good idea."

So I went in and said thank you to Rob's mom, who was sitting on the couch with Just-Call-Me-Gary watching TV in a snuggly sort of position that, had Rob seen it, might just have sent him over the edge. Fortunately, however, he did not see it. And I did not tell him about it, either.

"Well," I said to him, as I climbed behind the wheel of my mom's car. "Seeing as how we aren't broken up anymore, do you want to do something Saturday? Like go see a movie or whatever?"

"Gosh, I don't know," Rob said. "I thought you might be busy with your good friend Joanne."

"Look," I said. It was so cold out that my breath was coming out in little white puffs, but I didn't care. "My parents have a lot to deal with right now. I mean, there's the restaurant, and Mike dropping out of Harvard. . . ."

"You're never going to tell them about me, are you?" Rob's gray eyes bore into me.

"Just let me give them a chance to adjust to the idea," I said. "I mean, there's the whole thing with Douglas and his job, and Great-aunt Rose, and—"

"And you and the psychic thing," he reminded me, with just the faintest trace of bitterness. "Don't forget you and the psychic thing."

"Right," I said. "Me and the psychic thing." The one thing I could never forget, no matter how much I tried.

"Look, you better get going," Rob said, straightening up. "I'll follow behind, and make sure you get home okay."

"You don't have to—"

"Mastriani," he said. "Just shut up and drive."

And so I did.

Only it turned out we didn't get very far.

CHAPTER

4

Not, may I point here and now, because of my poor driving skills. As I think I've stated before, I am an extremely good driver.

But I didn't know that at first. That I wasn't being pulled over on account of my driving ability, or lack thereof. All I knew was one minute I was cruising along the dark, empty country road that ran from Rob's house back into town, with Rob purring along behind me on his Indian. And the next, I rounded a curve to find the entire road blocked off by emergency vehicles—county sheriff's SUVs, police cruisers, highway patrol . . . even an ambulance. My face was bathed in flashing red and white. All I could think was, *Whoa! I was only going eighty, I swear!*

Of course it was a forty-mile-an-hour zone. But come on. It was Thanksgiving, for crying out loud. There hadn't been another soul on the road for the past ten miles. . . .

A skinny sheriff's deputy waved me to the shoulder. I obeyed, my palms sweaty. *My God,* was all I could think. *All this because I was driving without a license? Who knew they were so strict?*

The officer who strolled up to the car after I pulled over was one I recognized from the night Mastriani's burned down. I didn't remember his name, but I knew he was a nice guy—the kind of guy who maybe wouldn't bust my chops too badly for driving illegally. He shined a flashlight first on me, then into the backseat of my mom's car. I hoped he didn't think the stuff my mom had in the backseat—boxes of cassette tapes by Carly Simon and Billy Joel, and some videos of romantic comedies she kept forgetting to return to Blockbuster—were mine. I am so not the Carly Simon, *Sleepless in Seattle* type.

"Jessica, isn't it?" the cop said, when I put the window down. "Aren't you Joe Mastriani's daughter?"

"Yes, sir," I said. I glanced in the rearview mirror and saw Rob pull up right behind me on his Indian. His long legs were stretched out so that his feet rested on the ground, keeping him and the bike upright while he waited for me to get waved through the roadblock. Rob was gazing out at the cornfield to the right of us. The brown, withered stalks were bathed in the flashing red-and-white lights from the dozen squad cars and ambulance parked alongside the road. A few yards deeper into the field, a giant floodlight had been set up on a metal pole, and was shining down on something that we couldn't see, with the tall corn in the way.

"Too bad you have to work on Thanksgiving," I said to the cop. I was trying to be way nice to him, on account of my not having a driver's license, and all. Meanwhile, my palms were now so sweaty, I could barely grip the wheel. I had no idea what happens to people caught driving without a license, but I was pretty sure it wouldn't be very nice.

"Yeah," the cop said. "Well, you know. Listen, we kinda got a situation over here. Where you coming from, anyway?"

"Oh, I was just having dinner over at my friend's house," I said, and told him the address of Rob's house. "That's him," I added, helpfully, pointing behind me.

Rob had, by this time, switched off his engine and gotten down from his bike. He strolled up to the police officer with his hands at his sides instead of in the pockets of his leather jacket, I guess to show he wasn't holding a weapon or anything. Rob is pretty leery of cops, on account of having been arrested before.

"What's going on, Officer?" Rob wanted to know, all casual-like. You could tell he, like me, was worried about the whole driving without a license thing. But what kind of police force would set up a roadblock to catch license-less drivers on Thanksgiving? I mean, that was going way above and beyond the call of duty, if you asked me.

"Oh, we got a tip a little while ago," the cop said to Rob. "Regarding some suspicious activity out here. Came out to have a look around." I noticed he hadn't taken out his little ticket book to write me up. *Maybe,* I thought. *Maybe this isn't about me.*

Especially considering the floodlight. I could see people traipsing out from and then back into the cornfield. They appeared to be carrying things, toolboxes and stuff.

"You see anything strange?" the police officer asked me. "When you were driving out here from town?"

"No," I said. "No, I didn't see anything."

It was a clear night. . . . Cold, but cloudless. Overhead was a moon, full, or nearly so. You could see pretty far, even though it was only about an hour shy of midnight, by the light of that moon.

Except that there wasn't much to see. Just the big cornfield, stretching out from the side of the road like a dark, rustling sea. Rising above it, off in the distance, was a hill covered thickly in trees. The backwoods. Where my dad used to take us camping, before Douglas got sick, and Mikey decided he liked computers better than baiting fishhooks, and I developed a pretty severe allergy to going to the bathroom out of doors.

People lived in the backwoods . . . if you wanted

to call the conditions they endured there living. If you ask me, anything involving an outhouse is on the same par with camping.

But not everyone who got laid off when the plastics factory closed was as lucky as Rob's mom, who found another job—thanks to me—pretty quickly. Some of them, too proud to accept welfare from the state, had retreated into those woods, and were living in shacks, or worse.

And some of them, my dad once told me, weren't even living there because they didn't have the money to move somewhere with an actual toilet. Some of them lived there because they *liked* it there.

Apparently not everyone has as fond an attachment as I do to indoor plumbing.

"When you drove through, coming from town," the police officer said, "what time would that have been?"

I told him I thought it had been after eight, but well before nine. He nodded thoughtfully, and wrote down what I said, which was not much, considering I hadn't seen anything. Rob, standing by my mom's car, blew on his gloved hands. It *was* pretty cold, sitting there with the window rolled down. I felt especially bad for Rob, who was just going to have to climb back on his motorcycle when we were through being questioned and ride behind me all the way into town and then back to his house, without even a chance to get warmed up. Unless of course I invited him into my mom's car. Just for a few minutes. You know. To defrost.

Suddenly I noticed that those police officers, hurrying in and out of that cornfield? Yeah, those weren't toolboxes they were carrying. No, not at all.

Suddenly my palms were sweaty for a whole different reason than before.

Let me just say that in Indiana, they are always finding bodies in cornfields. Cornfields seem to be the preferred dumping ground for victims of foul play by Midwestern killers. That's because until the farmer who owns the field cuts down all the stalks to plant new rows, you can't really see what all is going on in there.

Well, suddenly I had a pretty good idea what was going on in this particular cornfield.

"Who is it?" I asked the policeman, in a high-pitched voice that didn't really sound like my own.

The cop was still busy writing down what I'd said about not having seen anyone. He didn't bother to pretend that he didn't know what I was talking about. Nor did he try to convince me I was wrong.

"Nobody you'd know," he said, without even looking up.

But I had a feeling I did know. Which was why I suddenly undid my seatbelt and got out of the car.

The cop looked up when I did that. He looked more than up. He looked pretty surprised. So did Rob.

"Mastriani," Rob said, in a cautious voice. "What are you doing?"

Instead of replying, I started walking toward the harsh white glow of the floodlight, out in the middle of that cornfield.

"Wait a minute." The cop put away his notebook and pen. "Miss? Um, you can't go over there."

The moon was bright enough that I could see perfectly well even without all the flashing red-and-white lights. I walked rapidly along the side of the road, past clusters of cops and sheriff's deputies. Some of them looked up at me in surprise as I breezed past. The ones who did look up seemed startled, like they'd seen something disturbing. The disturbing thing appeared to be me, striding toward the floodlight in the corn.

"Whoa, little missy." One of the cops detached himself from the group he was in, and grabbed my arm. "Where do you think you're going?"

"I'm going to look," I said. I recognized this police officer, too, only not from the fire at Mastriani's. I recognized this one from Joe Junior's, where I sometimes bussed tables on weekends. He always got a large pie, half sausage and half pepperoni.

"I don't think so," said Half-Sausage, Half-Pepperoni. "We got everything under control. Why don't you get back in your car, like a good little girl, and go on home."

"Because," I said, my breath coming out in white puffs. "I think I might know him."

"Come on now," Half-Sausage, Half-Pepperoni said, in a kindly voice. "There's nothing to see.

Nothing to see at all. You go on home like a good girl. Son?" He said this last to Rob, who'd come hurrying up behind him. "This your little girl-friend? You be a good boy, now, and take her on home."

"Yes, sir," Rob said, taking hold of my arm the same way the police officer had. "I'll do that, sir." To me, he hissed, "Are you nuts, Mastriani? Let's go, before they ask to see your license."

Only I wouldn't budge. Being only five feet tall and a hundred pounds, I am not exactly a difficult person to lift up and sling around, as Rob had illustrated a couple of times. But I had gotten pretty mad upon both those occasions, and Rob seemed to remember this, since he didn't try it now. Instead, he followed me with nothing more than a deep sigh as I barreled past the police officers, and toward that white light in the corn.

None of the emergency workers gathered around the body noticed me, at first. The ones on the outskirts of the crime scene hadn't exactly been expecting gawkers this far out from town, and on Thanksgiving night, no less. So it wasn't like they'd been looking out for rubber neckers. There wasn't even any yellow emergency tape up. I breezed past them without any problem....

And then halted so suddenly that Rob, follow-ing behind, collided into me. His *oof* drew the attention of more than a few officers, who looked up from what they were doing, and went, "What the—"

"Miss," a sheriff's deputy said, getting up

from the cold hard soil upon which he'd been kneeling. "I'm sorry, miss, but you need to stand back. Marty? Marty, what are you thinking, letting people through here?"

Marty came hurrying up, looking red-faced and ashamed.

"Sorry, Earl," he said, panting. "I didn't see her, she came by so fast. Come on, miss. Let's go—"

But I didn't move. Instead, I pointed.

"I know him," I said, looking down at the body that lay, shirtless, on the frozen ground.

"Jesus." Rob's soft breath was warm on my ear.

"That's my neighbor," I said. "Nate Thompkins."

Marty and Earl exchanged glances.

"He went to get whipped cream," I said. "A couple of hours ago." When I finally tore my gaze from Nate's bruised and broken body, there were tears in my eyes. They felt warm, compared to the freezing air all around us.

I felt one of Rob's hands, heavy and reassuring, on my shoulder.

A second later, the county sheriff, a big man in a red plaid jacket with fleece lining came up to me.

"You're the Mastriani girl," he said. It wasn't really a question. His voice was deep and gruff.

When I nodded, he went, "I thought you didn't have that psychic thing anymore."

"I don't," I said, reaching up to wipe the moisture from my eyes.

"Then how'd you know"—He nodded down at Nate, who was being covered up with a piece of blue plastic—"he was here?"

"I didn't," I said. I explained how Rob and I had come to be there. Also how Dr. Thompkins had been over at my house earlier, looking for his son.

The sheriff listened patiently, then nodded.

"I see," he said. "Well, that's good to know. He wasn't carrying any ID, least that we could find. So now we have an idea who he is. Thank you. You go on home now, and we'll take it from here."

Then the sheriff turned around to supervise what was going on beneath the flood lamp.

Except that I didn't leave. I wanted to, but somehow, I couldn't. Because something was bothering me.

I looked at Marty, the sheriff's deputy, and asked, "How did he die?"

The deputy shot a glance at the sheriff, who was busy talking to somebody on the EMS team.

"Look, miss," Marty said. "You better—"

"Was it from those marks?" I had seen that there'd been some kind of symbol carved into Nate's naked chest.

"Jess." Now Rob had hold of my hand. "Come on. Let's go. These guys have work to do."

"What were those marks, anyway?" I asked Marty. "I couldn't tell."

Marty looked uncomfortable. "Really, miss," he said. "You'd better go."

But I didn't go. I couldn't go. I just stood there, wondering what Dr. Thompkins and his wife were going to do, when they found out what had happened to their son. Would they decide to move back to Chicago?

And what about Tasha? She seemed to really like Ernest Pyle High School, if her enthusiasm about the yearbook committee was any indication. But would she want to stay in a town in which her only brother had been brutally murdered?

And what was Coach Albright going to say when he learned he'd lost yet another quarterback?

"Mastriani." Rob was starting to sound desperate. "Let's go."

I didn't realize precisely why Rob was sounding so desperate until I turned around. That was when I very nearly walked into a tall, thin man wearing a long black coat and a badge that indicated that he was a member of the Federal Bureau of Investigation.

"Hello, Jessica," Cyrus Krantz said to me, with a smile that I'm sure he meant to be reassuring, but which was actually merely sickening. "Remember me?"

CHAPTER

5

It would be hard to forget Cyrus Krantz. Believe me, I've tried. He's the new agent assigned to my case. You know, on account of me being Lightning Girl and all.

Only Cyrus Krantz isn't exactly a special agent. He's apparently some kind of FBI director. Of special operations, or something. He explained the whole thing—or at least he tried to—to my parents and me. He came over to our house not long after Mastriani's burned down. He didn't bring a pie or anything with him, which I thought was kind of tacky, but whatever. At least he called first, and made an appointment.

Then he sat in our living room and explained to my parents over coffee and biscotti about this new program he's developed. It is a division of the FBI, only instead of special agents, it is manned by psychics. Seriously. Only Dr.

Krantz—yeah, he's a doctor—doesn't call them psychics. He calls them "specially abled" individuals.

Which if you ask me makes it sound like they must all take the little bus to school, but whatever. Dr. Krantz was very eager for me to join his new team of "specially abled" secret agents.

Except of course I couldn't. Because I am not specially abled anymore. At least, that's what I told Dr. Krantz.

My parents backed me up, even when Dr. Krantz took out what he called "the evidence" that I was lying. He had all these records of phone calls to 1-800-WHERE-R-YOU, the missing children's organization with which I have worked in the past, that supposedly came from me. Only of course all the calls, though they were from my town, were placed through pay phones, so there was no real way to trace who'd made them. Dr. Krantz wanted to know who else in town would know the exact location of so many missing kids—a couple hundred, actually, since that day I'd been hit by lightning.

I said you never know. It could be anybody, really.

Dr. Krantz made this big appeal to my patriotism. He said I could help catch terrorists and stuff. Which I admit would be pretty cool.

But you know, I am not really sure that is something I would like to subject my family to. You know, the vengeful wrath of terrorists,

peeved that I caught their leader, or whatever. I
mean, Douglas gets freaked by call-waiting. How
much would terrorists rock his world?

So I politely declined Dr. Krantz's invitation,
all the while insisting I was about as "specially
abled" as Cindy Brady.

But that didn't mean Dr. Krantz had given up.
Like his protégés—Special Agents Smith and
Johnson, who'd been pulled off my case and
whom I sort of missed, in a weird way—Dr.
Krantz wasn't about to take no for an answer. He
was always, it seemed, lurking around, waiting
for me to mess up so that he could prove I really
did still have my psychic powers.

Which was unfortunate, because he was neither as pretty as Special Agent Smith, or as fun to
tease as Special Agent Johnson. Dr. Krantz was
just . . .

Scary.

Which was why when I saw him there in that
cornfield, I let out a little shriek, and must have
jumped about a mile and a half into the air.

"Oh," I said, when I'd pulled myself together
enough to speak in a normal voice. "Oh, Dr.
Krantz. It's you. Hi."

"Hello, Jessica." Dr. Krantz has kind of an egg-
shaped head, totally bald on top, only you couldn't
tell just then, because he was wearing a hat pulled
down low over his eyes. I guess he thought this
made him look like Dr. Magneto, or something. He
seemed like the kind of guy who'd want to be compared to the *X-men*'s Dr. Magneto.

His gaze flicked over Rob, whom he'd met before, only not in my living room, of course.

"Mr. Wilkins," he said, with a nod. "Good evening."

"Evening," Rob said, and, letting go of my hand to grab my arm instead, he began pulling. "Sorry. But we were just leaving."

"Slow down," Dr. Krantz said, with a creaky laugh. "Slow down there, young man. I'd like a word with Miss Mastriani, if I may."

"Yeah?" Rob said. He was about as fond as scientists in the employ of the U.S. government as he was of cops. "Well, she doesn't have anything to say to you."

"He's right," I said, to Dr. Krantz. "I really don't. Bye."

"I see." Dr. Krantz looked faintly amused. "And I suppose it was only by coincidence that you stumbled across this crime scene?"

"As a matter of fact," I said, in some surprise, since for once I was telling the truth, "it was. I was just passing by on my way home from Rob's."

"And the fact that I overheard you tell those gentlemen over there that the victim happens to be your neighbor?"

I said, "Hey, you're the government operative, not me. You ought to know more about this than I do. I mean, I'd feel pretty bad if a kid got killed during my watch."

Dr. Krantz's expression did not change. It never does. So I wasn't sure whether or not my words hit home.

"Jessica," Dr. Krantz said. "I want to show you something."

We were standing a little ways away from the circle the police officers and sheriff's deputies had made around the blue tarp covering Nate's body. But the glare from the floodlight was bright enough that, even though it was nighttime, I could see the details in the photo Cyrus Krantz pulled from inside his coat with perfect clarity.

It was, I realized, the overpass Mrs. Lippman had been talking about at dinner. The one with the graffiti spray-painted onto it. The graffiti she'd assumed was a gang tag. I myself had never noticed it.

Looking at it then, in the cold white glow of the floodlight, I saw that the red squiggle—that's all it looked like to me—seemed vaguely familiar. I had seen it before. Only where? There is not a lot of graffiti in our town. Oh, sure, the occasional *Rick Loves Nancy* out by the quarry. Every once in a while someone with a little too much school spirit painted *Cougars Rule* on the side of our rival high school's gymnasium. But that was it as far as graffiti went. I couldn't think where I could possibly have seen that red squiggle before.

Then, all at once, it hit me.

On Nate Thompkins's chest.

"So it *is* gang related?" I asked, handing the photo back to Cyrus Krantz. The two Thanksgiving suppers I'd eaten weren't sitting too well in my stomach all of a sudden.

Dr. Krantz tucked the photo back where he'd

found it. "No," he said, rebuttoning his coat. Dr. Krantz was always very neat and tidy. At our house, he hadn't left a single crumb on his plate. And my mom's biscotti is pretty crumbly.

"This," he said, tapping the pocket that held the photo, "was a warning. That"—He nodded at the blue tarp—"is just the beginning."

"The beginning of what?" I asked. Mrs. Wilkins's pumpkin pie was definitely on its way back up.

"That," Cyrus Krantz said, "is what we're going to find out, I'm afraid."

Then he turned around and started striding from the cornfield, back to his long, warm car.

Wait, I wanted to call after him. *What can I do? What can I do to help?*

But then I remembered that I am not supposed to have my psychic powers anymore. So I couldn't really offer him my help.

Besides, what could I do? Nobody was missing.

Not anymore.

I didn't speed the rest of the way home. Not because I was afraid of getting caught, but because I was really afraid of what I was going to find when I pulled onto Lumbley Lane. Even the purr of Rob's motorcycle behind me—he followed me home—wasn't very reassuring.

When we pulled onto my street, I saw the flashing lights right away. The sheriff must have radioed in the information I'd given him, since there were already two squad cars parked outside the Thompkins house. As I pulled into our driveway, Dr. Thompkins was just opening the door to let in the officers who stood there, their hats in their hands. Neither of them turned around as Rob, with a wave to me, took off down the street, having successfully escorted me practically to my door.

My entire family had their faces pressed to the glass of the living room windows when I walked in. Well, everybody except for Douglas, who was probably hiding in his room (flashing lights are not among his favorite things: They tend to remind him of the several ambulance trips he has taken in his lifetime).

"Oh, Jess," my mom said, when she saw me. The dining room table was clear. Everyone except for Claire had left. "Thank God you're home. I was getting worried."

"I'm fine," I said.

"Where does this Joanne live, anyway?" my mom wanted to know. "You were gone for hours."

But I could tell she wasn't really interested in my answer. All of her attention was focused on the Hoadley—I mean, Thompkins—house across the street.

"Those poor people," she murmured. "I hope it isn't bad news."

"Ma," Mike said, in a sarcastic voice. "Two sheriff cars are parked in their driveway. You think they're there with good news?"

"Don't call me Ma," my mother said. Then she seemed to realize what everybody was doing.

She looked shocked. "Get away from the windows! It's shameful, spying on those poor people like this."

"We aren't spying, Antonia," Great-aunt Rose said. "We are merely looking out the window. There's no law against that."

"Mrs. Mastriani is right," Claire said primly, getting up off the couch. "It's wrong to peep through other people's windows."

Claire obviously had no clue that Mike had been spying on her through her windows with a telescope for years.

I could have told them, I guess. I mean about Nate. But the way it was, I had barely been able to make it home with my dinner intact. I wasn't all that eager to risk losing it again. Instead, I said, "I'm going to bed," and I started up the stairs to my room. Only my mother said good night, and she sounded pretty distracted.

Upstairs, I saw that Douglas's bedroom light was still on. I thumped on his door instead of just barging in, like I used to do. Douglas has gotten a lot better since starting his job in the comic book store. I figured I'd reward him by letting him have some privacy for a change. Mr. Goodhart says this is called positive reinforcement.

"Come in, Jess," Douglas said. He knew it was me by my thump. My mom taps all timidly, my dad knocks Shave-and-a-Haircut, and Mike never visits Douglas, if he can help it. So Douglas always knows when it's me.

"Hey," I said. Douglas was lying on his bed,

reading, as usual. Tonight it was the latest install-ment of *Superman*. "What time did everybody leave?"

"About an hour ago," he said. "Mr. and Mrs. Abramowitz had a big fight over where they're going to go for Christmas break, Aspen or Antigua."

"Must be nice," I said. The Abramowitzes are way rich.

"Yeah. Skip contributed by having an asthma attack. Between that and Aunt Rose, it was an evening to remember."

"Huh," I said.

He must have seen by my face that something was wrong, since he went, "What?"

I shook my head. For a minute, I'd been pic-turing Nate Thompkins, as I'd last seen him, life-less in that cornfield. "Oh," I said. "Nothing."

"Not nothing," Douglas said. "Tell me."

I told him. I didn't want to. All right, I did. But I shouldn't have. Douglas has never been what you'd call well. I mean, he was always the one the other kids picked on in school, at the park, wherever. You know the kind. The one they call Spaz and Tard and Reject. I had spent much of my young adulthood pounding on the faces of people who'd dared to make fun of my older brother for being different.

And that's all Douglas is. Not crazy. Not retarded. Just different.

When I was through, Douglas, who knows the truth about my "special ability"—but not about

Rob; no one knows the truth about Rob, except for Ruth who is, after all, my best friend—let out a big gush of air.

"Whoa," he said.

"Yeah," I said.

"Those poor people," he said, meaning the Thompkinses.

"Yeah," I said.

"I've seen the daughter," he said, meaning Tasha. "At the store."

"Really?" Somehow I could not picture shy, pretty Tasha Thompkins, always so conservatively dressed, in Underground Comix, where Douglas worked.

"She's into *Witchblade*," Douglas elaborated. He seemed really concerned. I mean, for Douglas. "What did it look like, anyway?"

He had thrown me. "What did what look like?"

"The symbol," Douglas said, patiently. "The one on Nate's chest."

"Oh," I said. I went over to his desk and drew it, not very expertly, on a pad of paper I found lying there. "Like this," I said, and handed it to him.

He took the pad and studied what I had drawn. When, after a minute, he continued to squint down at it, I said, "It's supposed to be a gang symbol, or something. It only makes sense if you're in the gang."

"This isn't a gang symbol," Douglas said. "I

mean, I don't think so. It looks familiar."

"Yeah," I said. "Because you've probably seen it before, driving under the overpass. Somebody spray-painted it there."

"I never go by the overpass," Douglas said. Then he did something really weird. I mean weird for Douglas.

He got out of bed and started pulling books off his shelves. Douglas has more books—and comic books—than anyone I know. Still, if you wanted to borrow one, and took it down off the shelf and forgot to mention it to him, Douglas would notice right away it was missing, even though there are maybe a thousand other ones that look exactly like it right there on the shelf beside it.

Douglas is one of those book people.

Seeing that he was going to be occupied until well into the night, I left. I doubted he even noticed. He was way too absorbed in looking things up.

In my own room, I undressed quickly, slipping into my pajamas—a pair of fleece warm-up pants and a long-sleeved tee—with lightning speed. That is because my room, which is on the third floor, is the draftiest room in the house, and from Halloween until Easter it is freezing, in spite of the space heater my dad had installed.

I don't mind the cold, however, because I have the best view of anybody from my bedroom windows, and that's including Mike, whose view into Claire Lippman's bedroom is what caused all that trouble a few months ago, when he decided to drop out of Harvard because he and Claire were in love. My view, which is from some dormer windows high above the treetops, is of all of Lumbley Lane, which in the moonlight always looks like a silver river, the sidewalks on either side of it mossy banks. In fact, when I'd been younger, I used to pretend Lumbley Lane was a river, and that I was the lighthouse operator, high above it. . . .

Whatever. I'd been a weird kid.

That night, as I undid Rob's watch, which he'd given me a few months earlier, and which I wore like an ID bracelet, (much to the bewilderment of my parents, who thought it was a bit odd that I went around with this bulky man's watch weighing my hand down all the time), I didn't look down at the street. I didn't pretend Lumbley Lane was a river, or that I was the lighthouse operator, guiding tempest-tossed ships safely to shore.

Instead, I looked across the street, into Tasha Thompkins's bedroom window. The lights in her room were still on. She had probably heard the news about her brother by now. I wondered if she was stretched out on her bed, crying. That's where I'd be, if I found out either of my brothers had been killed. I felt a wave of grief for Tasha, and for her parents. I didn't know anything about gangs, but I thought that whoever had killed Nate couldn't have known him all that well, because he'd been a nice kid. Smart, too. It was a waste. A real waste.

After a while, the front door to the Hoadley—

I mean, Thompkins—house opened, and Dr. Thompkins, looking much older than when I had seen him earlier that evening, came out, wearing his coat. He followed the sheriff's deputies to their squad cars, then got into one. I knew he was going to ID the body. At the front door, his wife stood watching him. I couldn't tell whether or not she was crying, but I suspected she was. Two people stood on either side of her. Nate's grandparents, I assumed.

Above them, I saw a curtain move. Tasha was standing in her window, looking down as the squad car with her father in it pulled away. I saw that Tasha's shoulders were shaking. Unlike her mother, she was definitely crying.

Poor, shy, yearbook-committee-and-*Witchblade*-loving Tasha. There was nothing I could do for her. I mean, if I had known when his father had come over that Nate was in trouble, I might have been able to find him. Maybe. But it was too late, now. Too late for me to help Nate, anyway.

But not too late, I realized, to help his sister. How I was going to do that, I hadn't the slightest idea.

All I could do was try.

Little did I know, of course, how my decision to help Tasha Thompkins was going to change my life. And the life of just about everybody in our entire town.

CHAPTER

6

The next day, when Ruth told me some kid from her synagogue was missing, I didn't make the connection. I had a lot on my mind. I mean, there was the whole thing with Nate Thompkins, of course. I hadn't forgotten about my promise to myself that I was going to try to help Tasha, if I could.

There was something else, though. Something I'd dreamed about that had been, well, pretty disturbing. Not as disturbing as having your brother left for dead in a cornfield, but still wicked strange.

"Are you listening to me, Jess?" Ruth wanted to know. She had to talk pretty loudly to be heard over the Muzak in the mall. We were hitting the post-holiday sales. Hey, it was the Friday after Thanksgiving. There was nothing else to do.

"Sure," I said, fingering a pair of hoop earrings on a nearby display rack. And I don't even have pierced ears. That's how distracted I was.

"They found his bike," Ruth said. "And that's it. Just his bike. In the parking lot. No other sign of him. Not his book bag. Not his clarinet. Nothing."

"Maybe he ran away," I said. The earrings, I thought, wouldn't make a bad Christmas present for Ruth. I mean, Hanukkah present. Because Ruth was Jewish, of course.

"No way Seth Blumenthal is going to run away before his thirteenth birthday," Ruth said. "He's supposed to be having his bar mitzvah tomorrow, Jess. That's what he was doing at the synagogue in the first place. Having his last Hebrew lesson before the big ceremony on Saturday. The kid is due to rake it in. No way would he take off beforehand. And no way would he leave his bike behind."

This finally got my attention. Twelve-year-olds do not generally abandon their bikes. Not without a fight, anyway. And Ruth was right: She'd pulled in roughly twenty thousand dollars for her bat mitzvah. No way some kid was going to run away before making that kind of dough.

"You got a picture of him?" I asked Ruth, as she worked her way through a Cinnabon she was carrying around. "Seth, I mean."

"There's one in the temple directory," she said. "I mean, it's a shot of his whole family. But I can point him out for you, if you want."

"Okay," I said. "I'll take care of it."

"Soon," Ruth said to me. "You better take care of it soon. There's no telling what might have happened to him. I mean, that gang might have gotten him."

I rolled my eyes. I actually had to keep a eye out, because I'd spotted my mother and Great-aunt Rose—horror of horrors—going into JC Penney, and I wanted to be sure to avoid running into them. I was fairly certain that if Great-aunt Rose hadn't been visiting, there'd have been no way my mom would be at the mall the day after one of her neighbors found out their kid was dead. But I suspected since the neighbor in question was the Thompkinses, my mom hadn't dared risk a sympathy visit, since Great-aunt Rose would have insisted on coming along. And knowing Rose, she'd have started in about the darkies, or something equally appalling.

She was leaving on Sunday. Which might as well have been forever, it seemed so far away.

"If I get a piece of his clothing," Ruth was asking me, "could you do that thing? You know, that thing you did with Shane? And Claire? Where you smel—"

She broke off with a cry of pain as I reached up and seized her by the back of the neck. She was so surprised, a piece of Cinnabon fell out of her mouth.

"I told you not to talk about that, remember?" I hissed at her. Over at Santa's Workshop—the day after Thanksgiving was the day Santa arrived at our local mall—a bunch of moms looked our way, disapproving . . . probably because we were still young and weren't saddled down with three whiny brats, but whatever. "The Feds are still following me around, you know. I bumped into Cyrus just last night."

"Ow," Ruth said, shrugging off my hand. "Leggo, you freak."

"I mean it," I said. "Just be cool."

"You be cool." Ruth adjusted her shirt collar. "Or try just being normal for a change. What is the matter with you, anyway? You've been acting like a freak all day."

"Gee, I don't know, Ruth," I said, in my most sarcastic tone. "Maybe it's just because last night I saw the mutilated body of the guy who used to live across the street lying mangled in a corn-field."

Ruth curled her upper lip. "God," she said. "Be a little gross, why don't you?" Then Ruth looked at me a little closer. "Wait a minute. You aren't blaming yourself over Nate's death, are you?" When I didn't reply, she went, "Oh my God. You *are*. Jess, hello? You didn't kill him, okay? His little gang-bang buddies did."

"I knew he was missing," I said. Over at Santa's Workshop some kid was screaming his head off because he was afraid of the mechanical elves building toys in the fake snow. "And I didn't try to find him."

"You knew he'd gone out for whipped cream," Ruth corrected me. "And that he didn't come back right away. You didn't know he was being murdered. You couldn't have known. Come *on*, Jess. Give yourself a break. You can't be responsible for every single person on the planet who gets himself killed."

"I guess not," I said. I turned away from the sight of the mall Santa ho-ho-hoing. "Look, Ruth, let's go home. You can show me that picture. So maybe if the bar-mitzvah boy really is missing, I can find him before he becomes crow fodder, the way Nate did."

"Eew," Ruth said. "Graphic much?" But she started heading toward the nearest exit.

Only not soon enough, unfortunately.

"Jessica!"

I turned at the sound of the familiar voice . . . then blanched.

It was Mrs. Wilkins. And Rob.

Just about the last two people—with the exception of my mom and Great-aunt Rose—I'd wanted to run into. Not because I wasn't happy to see them. Let's face it, when have I ever been unhappy about seeing Rob? That would be like being unhappy about seeing the sun come out after forty days and nights of rain.

But knowing what I knew now . . . what I'd learned overnight, as I slept, without consciously meaning to, and all because of that stupid picture I'd seen on Rob's mother's bedroom wall. . . .

"Hi, you guys," I said, brightly, to cover up what I was really feeling, which was, *Oh, shit.* "Wow. Fancy meeting you here." Again, among the most toolish of things to say, but I was trying to think fast.

Rob looked about as uncomfortable as I had ever seen him. This was on account of the fact that:

a)He was in a mall.
b)He was in a mall with his mom.
c)He had run into me there.
d)I was with Ruth.

Ruth and Rob are not among one another's favorite people. In fact, I had only recently convinced Ruth to stop referring to Rob as The Jerk on account of him never calling me. Rob thought Ruth was an elitist Townie snob who looked down on non-college-bound people such as himself. Which in fact she was. But that didn't make her a bad person, necessarily.

"Isn't this funny," Mrs. Wilkins said, with a happy smile. "I've been trying to convince Rob to let me take him to get measured for a tux for my brother's wedding since . . . well, forever, it seems like. And today, when he picked me up after work, he finally agreed. So here we are. And here you are! Isn't that funny?"

"It sure is," I said, even though I didn't think it was funny at all. Especially since Rob hadn't said anything to me about having a wedding to attend. A wedding at which he might be expected to bring a date. Who by rights should be have been me. "I thought Earl was already married," I said, to cover up my inner rage over Rob having never mentioned this before.

"Oh, it's not Earl," Mrs. Wilkins said. "It's my little brother Randy. He and his fiancée are tying the knot on Christmas Eve. Have you ever heard of anything so romantic?"

Christmas Eve? A Christmas Eve wedding at which Rob would be wearing a tuxedo, and he hadn't said a word to me about it? I'd have gone with him, if he'd asked me. I'd have gone with him gladly. I'd have worn the green velvet sheath dress my mom had made me for last year's Lion's Club dinner in honor of Mike winning that scholarship. If my mom wasn't around, wearing the one she'd made herself that matched mine, it actually looked good on me.

But no. No, Rob hadn't even bothered to mention he'd been invited to this affair. Nothing. Not a word.

Suddenly I felt like blurting out what I had learned in my dreams last night about Rob's dad, right in front of everyone, just to get back at him for having purposefully left me out of this very important family event that I was now dying to go to more than I had ever wanted to go to anything before in my life.

"How nice," I said, with what I hoped was a frosty smile in Rob's direction. He was studiously avoiding my gaze. Or maybe he was just trying to avoid making eye contact with Ruth, who was pointedly returning the favor. Either way, he was a dead man.

"Oh, but, Jess!" Mrs. Wilkins's hand shot out, and she grasped my fingers, the smile wiped from her face. "Rob told me what happened to you two on your way back home last night. I'm so sorry! It must have been awful. I feel so terrible for the boy's parents. . . ."

"Yes," I said, my smile growing less frosty. "It was pretty bad."

"If there's anything I can do," Mrs. Wilkins said. "I mean, I can't imagine how I could help, but if you think those poor people could use some home cooking, or something, let me know. I do make a decent casserole. . . ."

"Sure thing, Mrs. Wilkins," I said. "I'll let you know. And thanks again for dinner last night."

"Oh, honey, it was nothing," Mrs. Wilkins said, squeezing my fingers one last time before letting them go. "I'm just so glad you could share it with us."

All that would have been bad enough. But a second later, the whole thing got about ten times worse. Just when I thought I was about to escape virtually unscathed—except for the whole not-having-been-asked-to-Rob's-uncle's-wedding thing—I heard a sound that caused the blood in my veins to curdle.

Which was Great-aunt Rose, calling my name.

"See, I told you it was Jessica," Great-aunt Rose said, hauling my mother up to us. Rose's blue eyes, which appeared rheumy, but which actually took in everything around them with uncanny clarity, crackled as she looked from Rob to me and then back again. "Who is your little friend, Jessica? Aren't you going to introduce us?"

The idea of Great-aunt Rose, a tiny shrimp of a woman, calling Rob "little" would have made me laugh at any other time. As it was, however, I merely longed for the floor of the mall to open up and swallow me as quickly and as painlessly as possible.

My mother, looking tired and distracted—and who wouldn't, having spent the day with Great-aunt Rose—put down the many bags she was holding and said, "Oh, Mary. It's you. How are you?" My mom knew Mrs. Wilkins from the restaurant, of course.

"Hi, Mrs. Mastriani," Mrs. Wilkins said with her sunny smile. "How are you today?"

"Fair," my mom said, "to middling." She looked at me and Ruth. "Hello, girls. Any luck with the sales?"

"I got a cashmere sweater at Benneton," Ruth said, holding up a bag like a triumphant hunter, "for only fifteen dollars."

"It's chartreuse," I reminded her, before she could get too cocky.

"I'm sure it's very flattering," my mother said, just to be polite, because anyone who saw Ruth's blonde hair and sallow complexion would know chartreuse would not be flattering on her at all.

"And *you* are?" Great-aunt Rose asked Rob, pointedly.

Rob, God love him, carefully wiped off his hand on his jeans before extending it toward my aunt and going, in his deep voice, "Rob Wilkins, ma'am. Very nice to meet you."

Great-aunt Rose merely lifted her nose at the sight of Rob's hand. "And what are your intentions toward my niece?" she demanded.

Mrs. Wilkins looked startled. My mother looked confused. Ruth looked delighted. I am sure I looked like I had just swallowed a cactus. Only Rob remained calm, as he replied, in the same polite tone, "I have no intentions toward her at all, ma'am."

Which is exactly the problem.

I saw my mother's eyes narrow as she looked at Rob. I knew what she was going to say a second before it was out of her mouth.

"Wait a minute," she said. "I know you from somewhere, don't I?"

The sad part was, she did. But I wasn't about to let her stick around to figure out where. Because where she knew Rob from was the police station, the last time I'd been hauled in there for questioning . . . a connection I did not want my mother making just then.

"I'm sure you've just seen him around, Mom," I said, taking her by the arm and propelling her toward Santa's Workshop. "Hey, look, Santa's back! Don't you want to take my picture sitting on his lap?"

My mom looked down at me with mild amusement. "Not exactly," she said. "Considering you're no longer five years old."

Ruth, for once in her life, did something helpful, and came up on my mom's other side, saying,

"Aw, come on, Mrs. M. It would be so funny. My parents would crack up if they saw a picture of me and Jess on Santa's lap. And to get her back, I'll make Jess come to temple and sit on Hanukkah Harry's lap next week. Come on."

My mom looked helplessly at Mrs. Wilkins, who fortunately didn't seem aware that anything unusual—such as the fact that her son's supposed girlfriend was doing everything in her power to keep her mother from actually meeting him—was going on.

"Oh, go on," Mrs. Wilkins said, laughingly, to my mom. "It'll be a hoot."

My mom, shaking her head, let us steer her into the line to see Santa. It was only when I came back to say good-bye to Mrs. Wilkins—I was ignoring Rob—and to get the bags my mom had set down that I overheard Great-aunt Rose hiss at Rob, "Watch yourself, young man. I've seen your type before, and I'm warning you: Don't you even think about laying a finger on my niece. Not if you know what's good for you."

I glared at Great-aunt Rose. Just what I needed, for her to give Rob yet another excuse why he couldn't go out with me.

Rob seemed hardly to have heard her, however. Instead, he only looked at me, those smokey gray eyes unreadable. . . .

Almost. I was pretty sure I read something in the set of his square jaw. And that something said, *Thanks for nothing.*

It was only then that I realized I'd had a perfect chance finally to introduce him to my mother, and that, in my panic, I'd blown it.

But hey, who'd had the perfect chance to ask me to be his escort at his uncle Randy's Christmas Eve wedding, and blown that?

When I returned to the line to see Santa, with my mom's bags and Great-aunt Rose in tow, it was only to hear Ruth whisper in a low voice, *"You owe me."* It took me a minute to realize what Ruth meant. I heard snickering. Looking past the cottony field of fake snow that surrounded us, I saw Karen Sue Hankey and some of her cronies pointing at us and laughing their heads off.

I really don't think my mom should have gotten so mad over the gesture I made at them, despite the fact that there were small children around. They probably didn't even know what it meant. Great-aunt Rose sure didn't.

"No, Jessica," she informed me acidly, a second later. "The peace sign is with two fingers, not one. Don't they teach you children anything in school these days?"

CHAPTER

7

There were more cars than ever outside the Hoadley—I mean Thompkins—house when we got home from the mall later that afternoon.

I was surprised the Thompkinses were acquainted with that many people. For being so new in town, they were pretty popular.

"Look," Ruth said, as I got out of her car. "Coach Albright's there."

Sure enough, I recognized the coach's Dodge Plymouth. It was hard not to, as he'd had the car custom painted in the Ernie Pyle High School colors of purple and white.

"God," Ruth said, sympathetically, as I climbed out of her car. "Poor Tasha. Can you imagine having that blowhard in your living room the day after your brother got murdered? That has to be one of those circles of hell Dante was going on about." We are doing Dante's

Inferno in English. Well, everyone else is. I am mainly playing Tetris on my Gameboy in the back row with the sound off.

"Come over later with that picture," I said. "I mean, if the kid from your synagogue is still missing when you get home."

"He will be," Ruth said, bleakly. "This appears to be a day destined for human tragedy. I mean, look at my new sweater."

I slammed the car door shut and started across my yard, into the house. The snow that the Weather Channel had been talking about still hadn't appeared, but there was a thick layer of grayish-white clouds overhead. Not a hint of blue showed anywhere. And the wind was pretty nippy. My face, the only part of me exposed to the elements, practically froze during my twenty-foot walk from the driveway to our front door.

"Hey," I yelled, as I came in. "I'm home." It was safe to yell this, as Ruth and I had beaten my mom and Great-aunt Rose home from the mall. So the only people who might have heard me were people I didn't actually mind speaking to.

Only nobody answered my yell. The house appeared to be empty.

I walked over to the hall table to look at the mail. Christmas catalog, Christmas catalog, Christmas catalog. It was amazing how those Christmas catalogs piled up, starting before Halloween, even. Ours all went straight into the recycle bin.

A bill. Another bill. A letter from Harvard,

addressed to my parents, no doubt begging them to reconsider letting Mikey drop out. Like they'd had any choice in the matter. Mike had purchased a one-way ticket home the minute he'd heard his lady fair had been hospitalized on account of almost being murdered, and then had refused to go back once Claire turned the full force of her baby blues on him. (It's way cooler, Claire told me, to have a boyfriend in college than one who is still in high school. I guess even if that boyfriend is a Class A-certified geek.)

There was nothing in the mail for me. There is never anything in the mail for me. All of my mail—such as it is—gets sent to me secretly from my friend Rosemary at 1-800-WHERE-R-YOU via Ruth, who then smuggles it over. But Rosemary was in Rhode Island visiting her mother for Thanksgiving, so I wasn't expecting anything from her this week. The missing kids were just going to have to wait until next week to get found.

Except for Seth Blumenthal, if he really was missing.

Sighing, I pulled off my hat and gloves, stuffed them in my coat pockets, and went to hang up my coat by the door to the garage. A perusal of the fridge revealed that no one had been by recently with any interesting offerings in the form of food solace. I nibbled on some leftover persimmon pie, but my heart wasn't in it. You would think I'd have been standing there thinking about what was going on across the street. I mean about Nate, and all. A sixteen-year-old kid, killed before he'd ever even gotten his driver's license, and for what? Wearing the wrong gang's colors?

But of course I wasn't thinking about Nate at all. I was thinking about Rob, and how hurt he'd looked when I hadn't introduced him to my mom. Well, how hurt did he think I felt when I found out about that wedding he hadn't invited me to? He couldn't have it both ways. He couldn't insist that we can't go out because of our age difference, then be hurt when I didn't introduce him to my mom.

The two of us definitely had some problems in our relationship that needed working out. Maybe we needed to go on *Oprah*, and talk to that bald doctor dude she's always having on.

"Doctor, my girlfriend is ashamed of me," I could almost hear Rob saying. "She won't introduce me to her parents."

"Well, my boyfriend doesn't trust me," I would retort. "He won't tell me what he got arrested for. Or invite me to his uncle Randy's wedding."

Yeah. The two of us on *Oprah*. That was so going to happen.

It wasn't until I got upstairs that I heard the voices. I have to admit that my brother Douglas, even when he isn't having one of his episodes, has a tendency to talk to himself.

But this time, someone was talking back. I was sure of it. The door to his room was closed, as always, but I pressed my ear up to it, and there was no doubt about it: There were two voices coming from Douglas's room.

And one of them belonged to a *girl.*

I assumed it was Claire. Maybe she was consulting with Douglas over what to get Mike for a Christmas present. Or had gone to him for advice because their relationship had run into trouble. . . .

But why would she go to Douglas with something like that? Why not me? I was clearly the logical choice. I mean, I may be a freak and all, with my psychic powers, but I am way less of a freak than Douglas, much as I love him.

I couldn't help it. I knew I shouldn't, but I did it anyway. I thumped, once on the door, then threw it open.

"Hey, good lookin'," I started to say. "What's cookin'?"

Only it wasn't Claire in Douglas's room. It wasn't Claire at all.

It was Tasha Thompkins.

My jaw sagged so loose at the sight of her, sitting all primly on the end of Douglas's bed, in her black turtleneck and gray wool jumper, I swear I felt my chin hit the floor.

"Oh," she said, when she saw me, her tear-filled brown eyes soft as her voice. "Hi, Jess."

"Wh . . ." I said. I couldn't think of a single thing to say. Never in a million years would I have expected to open Douglas's bedroom door and find a girl in his room. Much less one to whom he wasn't related by blood, or who was dating his younger brother. "Wh . . . wh . . . wh . . ."

"Close the barn door," Douglas said mildly to me, from where he sat in front of his desktop computer. "You're letting the flies in."

I snapped my mouth shut. But I couldn't think of anything to say. I just stared at Tasha, looking neat and pretty and strangely not out of place in Douglas's book- and comic book-filled bedroom.

"I just couldn't take it anymore," Tasha said, helping me out a little. "At our house, I mean. It's just so . . . Well, Coach Albright is there right now."

"I saw his car," I managed to croak.

"Yes," Tasha said. "Well. I couldn't stand it. Then I remembered that the last time I'd seen Doug, he'd said he had some really early issues of a comic book I like, and that I could come over sometime to see them." She shrugged her slender shoulders. "So I came over." When I didn't say anything, and just continued to stare at her, she said, looking vaguely troubled, "That's all right with you, isn't it, Jessica?"

I tried to say yes, but what came out was some kind of garbled noise like Helen Keller made in that movie about her life. So I just nodded instead.

"Don't worry about Jess," Douglas said. "She's just shy."

That made Tasha laugh a little. "That's not what I heard," she said. Then she looked guilty. For laughing, though, not because of what she'd said.

"I was asking Tasha about Nate," Douglas said casually, as if he were continuing a conversation that had gotten interrupted.

I tried to make an effort to speak intelligently. "I'm sorry," was all I managed to get out. When Tasha just looked at me, I went, "About your brother, I mean."

Tasha looked down at her shoes. "Thank you," she said, so softly, I could barely hear her.

"It turns out," Douglas said, after clearing his throat, "that Nate had a few unsavory friends."

Tasha nodded, her expression grave. "But they wouldn't have done this," she explained. "I mean, killed him. They were just a bunch of hop-heads who thought they were all that, you know?"

When both Douglas and I looked at Tasha blankly, she elaborated. Apparently, it isn't just that Chicagoans say hello instead of hey. They have a whole separate language unto themselves.

"They were the bomb," Tasha explained. "They ruled the school."

"Oh," I said. Douglas looked even more confused than I felt.

"It was all so lame," Tasha said, shaking her head so that the curled ends of her hair, held back in a second clip at the nape of her neck, swept her shoulders. "I mean, the only reason they wanted Nate around was because of Dad. You know. Prescription pads and all. Oxy makes for a wicked weekend high."

I nodded like I knew what she was talking about.

"But Nate, he was flattered, you know? I tried to tell him those guys were just using him, but he wouldn't listen. Fortunately it wasn't long before my dad found out. Nate had always been a good student, you know? So when his grades started to slip . . ." Tasha stared at a *Lord of the Rings* poster on Douglas's wall, but it was clear she wasn't seeing it. She was seeing something else entirely.

"My dad was so mad," she went on, after a minute, "that he pulled us both out of school. He took the job down here the very next day. We moved that week."

Whoa. Talk about tough love.

But I guess I could understand Dr. Thompkins's point of view. I mean, my family's had problems for sure, but drugs have never been one of them.

"So." I didn't want to bring up what was clearly going to be a painful subject for her, but I didn't see how it could be avoided. "Is that what happened to him, then? Your brother, I mean? Those, um, hopheads got him? For not giving them any more prescription pads, or something?"

Tasha shook her head, looking troubled.

"I don't know," she said. "I mean, those guys were bad news, but they weren't killers."

I thought for a minute.

"What about that symbol?"

Douglas, over by the desk, was making a slashing motion with his hand beneath his chin. But it was too late.

Tasha looked at me blankly. "What symbol?"

I had blown it. Tasha didn't know. Tasha didn't know the details of her brother's death.

"Nothing," I said. "Just . . . um. There's been

some graffiti popping up around town, and some people were speculating that it was a gang tag."

"You think my brother was in a gang?" Tasha asked, in an incredulous voice.

Douglas dropped his forehead into one hand, as if he couldn't bear to watch.

"Well," I said. I couldn't tell her the truth, of course. About the symbol having been carved into her brother's chest. "That's kind of the rumor."

Tasha may not have been able to see things up close without the aid of prescription lenses, but she could see things far away without any problem. She glared at me pretty hard.

"Because he's black," she said, in a hard voice. "People assumed Nate was in a gang, and that he was the one going around tagging things, because he's black."

"Um," I said, throwing an alarmed look at Douglas. "Well, not exactly. I mean, you even said he was hanging out with, um, a bad element. . . ."

"For your information," Tasha said, standing up. Like almost everyone else in the world, she was taller than me. "That bad element happened to be, for the most part, white. We did not, as you seem to think, move here from the ghetto, you know."

"Look," I said, defensively. "I never said you did. All I said was that it's weird this symbol would start cropping up around town the same time that you happened to move here, and I was merely wondering if—"

"If we brought the criminal element down with

us from the big, bad city?" Tasha reached down and grabbed her coat, which had been draped across the bed beside her. "You know, the police have been asking us the same kind of questions. They all want to believe the same thing you do, that my brother deserved to be killed because of who he associated with. Well, I've got news for the cops in this town, and for you, too, Jessica. It wasn't some evil street gang from the big city that murdered my brother. It was a homegrown killer all your own."

With that, she stomped from Douglas's room. It wasn't until we heard the front door slam shut behind her that Douglas started to applaud.

"Way to go," he said to me. "Have you ever considered a career in the diplomatic corp?"

I sank down onto the spot on Douglas's bed Tasha had vacated. "Oh, bite me."

Noting my dour expression, Douglas said, "Aw, cheer up. She'll get over it. She just lost her brother, after all."

"Yeah, and I really helped," I said. "Implying he was a gang-banger who might have had it coming."

"You didn't imply that," Douglas said. "Besides, I was basically asking her the same thing when you walked in."

"Yeah, well, I notice she didn't fly off the handle at *you*."

"Well," Douglas said. "Who could? Considering my personal charm, and all."

But I noticed a slight redness to his cheeks that hadn't been there before.

"Whoa," I said, sitting up straight. "Douglas!"

He looked at me warily. "What?"

"You like her! Admit it!"

"Of course I like her." Douglas turned back to his computer, and began to type rapidly. Douglas can out-type even Mikey, when he puts his mind to it. "She seems like a very nice person."

"No, but you *really* like her," I said. "You *like* like her."

Douglas stopped typing. Then he turned around in his computer chair and said, "Jess, if you tell anyone, I will kill you."

I rolled my eyes. "Who am I going to tell? So, why don't you ask her out?"

"Well, for one thing," Douglas said, "because thanks to you, she now hates my guts."

I took umbrage at that. "You said she'd get over it!"

"I was only saying that to make you feel better. Face it. You ruined it."

"Oh, no way." I got up off the bed. "You are not pegging her not wanting to go out with you on me. Not when you haven't even asked her yet. Why don't you ask her to go to a movie tomorrow night? One of those weird independent films comic book freaks like you are always going to."

"Um," Douglas said. "Let me see. Because her brother just got murdered?"

"Oh, yeah," I said, crestfallen. Then I brightened. "But you could ask her as a friend. I mean, she must be going crazy over there, with Coach Albright hanging around. I bet she'd say yes."

"I'll think about it," Douglas said, and turned back to his computer. "About your symbol. I've been researching it all day, but I haven't been able to come up with anything about it. Are you sure you drew it right?"

"Of course I'm sure," I said. "Douglas, I'm serious, you should totally ask her out."

"Jess," he said, to his monitor. "She's in high school."

Memories of Rob and me, in the barn the night before, came flooding back. But I shoved them firmly aside.

"So?" I said. "She's a senior, and mature for her age. You're immature for yours. It's a perfect match."

"Thanks," Douglas said, deprecatingly.

At that moment, I heard Ruth's voice calling my name. As was our custom, she had let herself into the house.

"I got that stuff," she said, appearing in the doorway a minute later, breathless and covered with flakes of snow. I guess the Weather Channel had been right after all. "On Seth Blumenthal. You know, that kid who disappeared this morning. Oh, hey, Douglas."

"Hey," Douglas said to Ruth, not making eye contact with her, as was *his* custom.

"Was that Tasha Thompkins I just saw leaving here?" Ruth wanted to know.

"Yes," I said. "That was her all right."

"I didn't know you two were so friendly," Ruth said to me, as she began to unwind her scarf from her neck. "That was nice of you to ask her over."

"I didn't," I said.

Ruth looked confused. "Then what was she doing here?"

"Ask *him*," I said, tilting my head in Douglas's direction.

He ducked back over his computer, but I could still see the tips of his ears reddening.

"What's a guy have to do," he wanted to know, "to get some privacy around here?"

CHAPTER

8

When I woke up the next morning, I knew where Seth Blumenthal was.

And where Seth Blumenthal was wasn't good. It wasn't good at all.

Having the psychic power to find anyone, anyone at all, isn't an easy thing to live with. I mean, look at how, just by seeing his picture on the wall of Mrs. Wilkins's bedroom, I now knew this thing about Rob's dad. I would have traded anything in the world not to have been in possession of that little piece of information, let me tell you.

Just as I would have traded anything in the world not to have to do what I knew I had to next.

No big deal, right? Just pick up the phone and dial 911, right?

Not. So not.

Normally when I am contacted about a missing kid, it goes like this: I make sure, before I call anyone, that the kid really does want to be found. This is on account of how once I found a kid who was way better off missing than with his custodial parent, who was a bonafide creep. Ever since then, I have really gone out of my way to make sure the kids I find aren't better off missing.

But in Seth's case, there was no question. No question at all.

But I couldn't simply pick up the phone, dial 911, and go, "Oh, yeah, hi, by the way, you'll find Seth Blumenthal on blankity-blank street; hurry up and get him, his mom's missing him a lot," and hang up, click.

Because ever since this whole psychic thing started, and the U.S. government began expressing its great desire to put me on the payroll, I've been having to pretend like I don't have my powers anymore. So how would it look if I called 911 from my bedroom phone and went, "Oh, yeah, Seth Blumenthal? Here's where to find him."

Not cool. Not cool at all.

So I had to get up and go find a pay phone somewhere so that at least I could give the semblance of a denial the next time Cyrus Krantz accuses me of lying about my "specially abledness."

But let me tell you, if there'd ever been a day I considered giving up on the whole subterfuge thing, it was this one. That's because when I stumbled out of my bed, heading for the space heater I always turned off before I went to sleep, only to wake with ice chips practically formed in my nostrils, I happened to look out the window, and noticed that Lumbley Lane was completely carpeted in white.

That's right. It had started snowing around four in the afternoon the day before, and apparently, it had not stopped. There had to be a foot and a half at least of fluffy white stuff already on the ground, and more was falling.

"Great," I muttered, as I hastily donned an extra pair of socks and all the flannel I could find. "Just great."

With that much snow, there'd naturally be a hush over everything outside. But there seemed to be an equal silence inside the house. As I came down the stairs, I noticed that neither Douglas nor Mikey's rooms were occupied. And when I got to the kitchen, the only person sitting there, unfortunately, was Great-aunt Rose.

"I hope you don't think you're going to go out looking like that," she said, over the steaming cup of coffee she was holding. "Why, you look like you just pulled some old clothes on over your pajamas."

Since this was exactly what I had done, I was not exactly ruffled by this statement.

"I'm just going to the convenience store," I said. I went over to the mudroom and started tugging on some boots. "I'll be right back. You want anything?"

"The convenience store?" Great-aunt Rose looked shocked. "You have a refrigerator stocked with every kind of food imaginable, and you still can't find something to eat? What could you possibly need from the convenience store?"

"Tampons," I said, to shut her up.

It didn't work, though. She just started in about toxic shock syndrome. She'd seen an episode of *Oprah* about it once.

"And by the time they got to her," Great-aunt Rose was saying, as I stomped around, looking for a pair of mittens, "her uterus had fallen out!"

I knew someone whose uterus I wished would fall out. I didn't say so, though. I pulled a ski cap over my bed-head hair and went, "I'll be right back. Where is everybody, anyway?"

"Your brother Douglas," Great-aunt Rose said, "left for that ridiculous job of his in that comic book store. What your parents can be thinking, allowing him to fritter away his time in a dead-end job like that, I can't imagine. He ought to be in school. And don't tell me he's sick. There isn't a single thing wrong with Douglas except that your parents are coddling him half to death. What that boy needs isn't pills. It's a swift kick in the patootie."

I could see why none of Great-aunt Rose's own kids ever invited her over anymore for the holidays. She was a real joy to have around.

"What about my mom and dad?" I asked. "Where are they?"

"Your father went to one of those restaurants of his," Great-aunt Rose said, in tones of great disapproval. Restauranting was probably, in her opinion, another example of time frittered away. "And your other brother went with your mom."

"Oh, yeah?" I pulled on the biggest, heaviest coat I could find. It was my dad's old ski parka. It was about ten sizes too big for me, but it was warm. Who cared if I looked like Nanook of the North? I certainly wasn't trying to impress the guys at the Stop and Shop. "Where'd they go?"

"To the fire," Great-aunt Rose said, and turned back to the newspaper that was spread out in front of her. LOCAL RESIDENT FOUND DEAD, screamed the headline. FOUL PLAY SUSPECTED. Uh, no duh.

I thought Great-aunt Rose had finally gone round the bend. You know, Alzheimer's. Because the fire that had burned down the restaurant had been nearly three months ago.

"You mean Mastriani's?" I asked. "They went to the job site?" It didn't make much sense that they'd go there, especially on a day like today. The contractors who were rebuilding the restaurant had knocked off for the winter. They said they'd finish the place in the spring, when the ground wasn't so hard.

So what were my mom and Michael doing at an empty lot?

"Not that fire," Great-aunt Rose said, disparagingly. "The new one. The one at that Jewish church."

Now Great-aunt Rose had my full attention. I stared at her dumbfounded. "There's a fire at the synagogue?"

"Synagogue," Great-aunt Rose said. "That's what they call it. Whatever. Looks like a church to me."

"There's a *fire* at the synagogue?" I repeated, more loudly.

Great-aunt Rose gave me an irritated look. "That's what I said, didn't I? And there's no need to shout, Jessica. I may be old, but I'm not—"

Deaf, is what she probably said. I wouldn't know, since I booked out of there before she could finish her sentence.

A fire at the synagogue. This was not a good thing. I mean, not that I go to temple, not being Jewish.

Still, Ruth and her family go to temple. They go to temple a lot.

And if the fire was big enough that my mom and Mikey had felt compelled to go . . .

Oh, yes. The fire was big enough. I saw the dark plume of smoke in the air before I even got to the end of Lumbley Lane. This was not good.

I slogged through the snow, heading for the Stop and Shop, which was fortunately in the same direction as the synagogue. They have plows in my town, but it takes forever for them to get around to the residential streets. They do all the roads around the hospital and courthouse first, then the residential areas . . . if they don't have to go back and do the important roads again, which, in a storm like this, they'd need to. They never bothered with rural routes at all. A big storm tended to guarantee that everyone who lived outside the city limits was snowed in for days. Which was good for kids—no school—but not so good for adults, who had to get to work. Lumbley Lane had not been plowed. Only our driveway had been shoveled. Mr. Abramowitz, the champion shoveler in the neighborhood, had barely made a dent in his driveway. . . . Only enough had been shoveled so that he could get the car out, undoubtedly so that he and his family could head over to the synagogue and see what they could do to help, the way my mom and Mikey had. In a small town, people tend to pitch in. This can be a good thing, but it can also be a bad thing. For instance, people are also eager to pitch in with the latest gossip. Which—case in point, Nate Thompkins—was not always so helpful.

By the time I got to the Stop and Shop, which was only a few streets away from my house, I was panting from the exertion of wading through so much snow. Plus my face felt frozen on account of the wind whipping into it, despite my dad's voluminous hood.

Still, I couldn't go inside to warm up. I had a call to make on the pay phone over by the air hose.

"Yeah," I said, when the emergency operator picked up. "Can you please let the police know that the kid they've been looking for, Seth Blumenthal, is at Five-sixty Rural Route One, in the second trailer to the right of the Mr. Shaky's sign?"

The operator, stunned, went, "What?"

"Look," I said. This was really just my luck. You know, getting a brain-dead emergency services operator, on top of a freaking snowstorm. "Get a pen and write it down." I repeated my message one more time. "Got it?"

"But—"

"Good-bye."

I hung up. All around me, the snow was swirling like millions of tiny ballerinas in fluffy white tutus. You know, like in that *Fantasia* movie. Or maybe those were milkweed pod seeds. Whatever. Any other time, it would have been pretty.

As it was, however, it was a huge pain in my ass.

I could have gone inside the Stop and Shop and warmed up, but I decided against it. It would be just my luck if Luther—Luther had worked the Saturday morning shift at the Stop and Shop since I'd been a little kid, and I had gone down there religiously every weekend to blow my allowance on licorice and Bazooka Joe—remembered I'd been there. When Cyrus came around and started asking questions, I mean, after Seth Blumenthal got found. Luther had a memory like a steel trap. He could name every race Dale Earnhardt had ever won.

The snow and wind were pretty bad, but they weren't blizzard level. You could get around, it was just really awkward. If I'd had a car, though, it probably would have been about as bad. I mean, I'd have made just about as much progress.

By the time I finally got to the synagogue, the wind had died down a little. There was still that eery silence, though, that you get when everything is carpeted in snow . . . this in spite of all the fire engines and men running with hoses. I spied my mom standing in the synagogue parking lot—all the snow there had melted on account of the flames and the water from the fire trucks— with Mikey and the Abramowitzes. I picked my way across the maze of hoses on the ground and came up to them.

"What is it with this town," I asked my mom, "and buildings going up in flames?"

"Oh, honey," my mom said, slipping an arm around me. "What are you doing here? You didn't walk all this way, did you?"

"Sure," I said, with a shrug. "Anything to get away from Aunt Rose."

My mom fingered my hood distractedly. "Why are you wearing Daddy's old coat?" she wanted to know. But I didn't have a chance to reply, because Michael punched me on the arm.

"So you finally decided to join us, huh?" he said.

"Yeah," I said. "Thanks for waking me up."

"I tried," Michael said. "You were dead to the world. Plus it looked like you were having one hell of a nightmare."

He wasn't kidding. Only it hadn't been my nightmare. It had been Seth Blumenthal's reality.

Ruth, standing there with her brother and parents, looked miserable. Her nose was red, and tears were streaming down her face. I didn't think from the cold, either.

"Are you okay?" I asked her.

"Not really," Ruth said. "I mean, I've been better."

"Oh, Jess." Mrs. Abramowitz noticed me for the first time. "It's you." I guess she hadn't recognized me right away with my dad's ski parka on. "Isn't it awful?"

Awful wasn't the word for it. The building was almost completely destroyed. Only a couple of interior walls still stood. The rest was just charred rubble, black against the whiteness of the snow.

"They couldn't get here fast enough to save it," Mrs. Abramowitz said, wiping a tear from where it dangled off the end of her nose. "On account of the ice."

"Now, Louise," my mom said, reaching out to give Mrs. Abramowitz's shoulders a squeeze. "Remember what you told me when it was the restaurant that was burning. It's the people that matter, not the building."

"Right," Mr. Abramowitz said. He and Skip were standing there with some other men, huddled in the wind. "No one got hurt. And that's what's important."

"No," Mrs. Abramowitz said, mournfully. "But . . . but the Torah. It's just *too* awful."

I looked questioningly at Ruth.

"The Torah," she explained. "You know, the holy scrolls. They think that's what they lit on fire first."

"They?" I stared at her. "What are you talking about? Someone *set* this fire? On *purpose?*"

"Judge for yourself," Ruth said, and pointed.

Following the direction of her gloved hand, I looked. Across the street from the synagogue stood our town's only Jewish cemetery. Because there aren't a whole lot of Jews in southern Indiana—there are more churches here than there are McDonalds, for sure—the cemetery was pretty small.

So it had been pretty easy for whoever had gone to town on it to knock over every single headstone.

Oh, yes. Every single one. Except of course the mausoleums, which they couldn't knock over. But they'd satisfied themselves by spray-painting those with swastikas. Swastikas and something else. Something that looked familiar.

It took me a minute, but finally, I recognized it: the symbol I'd seen on Nate Thompkins's chest.

CHAPTER

9

"It's a gang," Claire said.

"It's not a gang, all right?" I was pacing up and down the hallway outside Michael's room. "Nate Thompkins wasn't in a gang."

"Just because his sister doesn't want to believe it," Michael pointed out, "doesn't mean it isn't true."

"She said all they wanted to do was scam prescription drugs," I said. "Does what happened over at the synagogue look like the work of people whose primary interest is in partying?"

I threw an aggravated look at the two of them, but it was no good. They refused to get as upset about it as I was. This was partly because Claire was sitting in Michael's lap. I guess it's hard to get upset about murder, arson, and bias crimes going on in your own town while you're getting cozy with that special someone.

"Grits, then," Claire said, with a shrug.

I blinked at her. "I beg your pardon?"

"Well, think about it," Claire said. "We were all so worried when the Thompkinses moved in, that the Grits were going to try something. You know, burn a cross on their lawn, or whatever. Maybe the Grits did it. Killed Nate."

Michael brightened. "Hey," he said. "Yeah. And Grits hate Jews, too."

"Oh, my God." I stared at them. "Would you two stop? Grits couldn't have done any of this."

"Why not?" Claire asked. "When we had to read *Malcolm X* in World Civ, a lot of the Grits wouldn't do it, because they said they wouldn't read a book written by a black person. Only they didn't say black," she added, meaningfully.

"And I heard a Grit," Michael said, "at the grocery store the other day, going on about how the Holocaust never happened, and was all made up by the Jews."

"Would you two cut it out?" I couldn't believe what I was hearing. "Not all Grits are like that."

"She just says that," Michael said confidently to Claire, "because she's dating one."

Claire looked at me with bright-eyed interest. "You *are*? Oh, my God, Jess! That's so politically correct of you. But does he talk about NASCAR racing all the time? Because that would really bore me after a while."

I tried to give Michael the same kind of evil death glare Great-aunt Rose had down so perfect.

"Don't try to blame all this on the Grits," I said.

"The Grits have been around a long time, and so has the synagogue, and we never had a problem like this before."

Michael looked thoughtful. "Well," he said. "That's true enough."

"Grits are, for the most part, hard-working people," I said, "who haven't had the same advantages as us. It's wrong to blame them for every bad thing that happens in this town just because they happen to have less money than we do."

Claire went, "Well, there's only one explanation, then. It has to be Nate's gang."

I rolled my eyes. I couldn't believe we were back to square one all over again.

Fortunately at that moment footsteps sounded on the stairs. We turned to see Douglas, covered from head to toe in protective outerwear, but looking chilled to the bone nonetheless, come staggering into the hallway. His face, the only part of him that wasn't covered, was flushed. There were snowflakes in his eyelashes.

"Where have *you* been?" I demanded.

"Nowhere," Douglas said, with deceptive innocence, as he reached up to pull off his knit ski cap. His hair, beneath the cap, was sweaty looking, and stuck up at weird angles. He looked like a demented snowplow driver.

"What?" Michael said. "Did Dad corner you about the driveway?"

"Uh, yeah," Douglas said, ducking into his room. "Yeah, that's where I was."

He shut the door, so we were all looking at the DO NOT DISTURB sign he'd pinned up there.

Mike glanced at me. "Do we start worrying about him now," he wanted to know, "or later?"

The phone rang. I didn't rush to pick it up, or anything, since no one but Ruth ever calls me. And I knew Ruth wasn't home. She and her family had gone over to their rabbi's house, to try to console him over the loss of the Torah, which turned out to be a really bad thing. Like someone coming in and burning your Bible, only worse, because Torahs are harder to replace.

So you can imagine my surprise when my mom called up the stairs, "Jess, it's for you. Your friend Joanne."

Which would have been fine, of course. Except that I have no friend named Joanne.

"Hello?" I said curiously, after picking up the extension in Mike's room.

"Mastriani." It was Rob. Of course it was Rob. Who else would call me, pretending to be someone named Joanne?

"Oh," I said, watching with a fair amount of disgust as Mikey and Claire started kissing. Right there in front of me. Granted, it was Mike's room, and I guess he could do what he wanted to in it, but excuse me, ew. "Hey."

"Listen. About tonight," Rob said, in his deep voice. I wondered how he'd managed to fool my mom into thinking he was someone named Joanne. Had he spoken in falsetto? Or had he had his mom ask for me? Surely not. I mean, then he'd have had to admit to his mom that I hadn't told my parents about him. And that was something I was pretty sure Rob wasn't going to admit to anybody.

"You still want to do something?" Rob asked.

I prickled immediately. "What do you mean, do I still want to do something? Of course I still want to do something. We're going out, right? I mean, aren't we?"

Mikey and Claire, distracted by my tone of voice, which had suddenly gotten a little shrill, stopped kissing, and looked at me.

"Is that the Grit?" Claire mouthed, excitedly. I turned my back on them.

"Well," Rob said. "I don't know. I mean, yesterday at the mall, you seemed to wig out a little."

"I did not wig out," I said, appalled. "That was not wigging out. That was just . . . I mean, come on. That was weird. I mean, your mom, my mom. Whatever."

"Right," Rob said. But he didn't sound very convinced. "Whatever."

"But of course I still want to go out tonight," I said. I was clutching the phone very tightly, so tightly my knuckles were white. "I mean, if you want to. Go to dinner. Or a movie." Or to your uncle's Christmas Eve wedding. Whichever. Or both, actually.

"Well," Rob said, stretching that single syllable out unbelievably far. I hung onto the receiver in breathless anticipation. This was, I knew, ridiculous. Ruth would have killed me for it, if she'd known. Ruth has very firm rules about boys, and one of the rules is that you should never, ever chase them. Let the boys come to you.

And even though Ruth isn't what you'd call your stereotypical babe, the whole rules thing seemed to work pretty well for her.

But then again, as far as I know, Ruth isn't going out with a high school graduate who happens to have a criminal record.

Before Rob could say another word, however, the call waiting went off, as it usually did, right when I least wanted it to. I said to Rob, "Hold on. I've got another call." I tried to make it sound like this other call might conceivably be from one of the many other boys I knew who were just dying to take me out, but I don't know if I did a very convincing job. Especially since the only other boy I happen to know who wanted to take me out was Skip from next door, but Saturday nights he's always busy grand-wizarding the neighborhood Dungeons and Dragons game, so it probably wasn't him.

So, not surprisingly, when I pressed the receiver, the voice I heard on the other line was not Skip's. But I was far from expecting to hear from the person to whom it belonged.

"Jessica," Dr. Cyrus Krantz said. He sounded agitated. "We've got a problem."

You think you've got problems? I wanted to say. *I got a guy on the other line who apparently isn't aware that I am the best thing that ever happened to him.*

Instead, I said, "Oh?" like I couldn't imagine

what he was talking about. Even though I had a pretty good idea. He was calling about Nate Thompkins and the synagogue.

Only it turned out he wasn't. He was calling about something I'd almost managed to forget about . . . almost, because it was so horrible, I doubted I'd ever fully be able to forget it.

"Seth Blumenthal," he said, heavily. "We missed him, Jessica."

I felt something inside my head explode. The next thing I knew, I was screaming into the phone like a maniac.

"What do you mean, you missed him?" I shouted.

It was only when I saw the expressions on Mike's and Claire's faces that I realized what I'd just done.

Outed myself. Officially. To the head of the psychic network of the Federal Bureau of Investigation.

I felt all the blood run out of my face. Could my day, I wondered, possibly get worse?

"The officers who were dispatched to the scene," Dr. Krantz was saying, in my ear, "were unprepared for the amount of resistance they received from the—"

"Resistance?" I blurted, once again forgetting, in my indignation, that the call I'd made concerning Seth Blumenthal was supposed to have been anonymous. "What are you talking about, resistance? All they had to do was go in and get the kid and come out again. How hard is that?"

"Jessica." Dr. Krantz sounded strange. "They were fired upon."

"Well, of course they were," I practically shouted. "Because the people who took Seth Blumenthal against his will are criminals, Dr. Krantz. That's who tends to kidnap kids. Criminals. And that's what criminals do when the police show up. They try to evade capture."

"You failed to mention," Dr. Krantz said, "that Seth was being held against his will when you spoke to the nine-eleven operator, Jessica. You failed to mention—"

"That he'd been tied up and gagged and shut up in the linen closet of a double-wide? I guess I did fail to mention that, didn't I?" I could feel tears welling up beneath my eyelids. Crying. I was *crying*. "Maybe because I had to keep that call short, in the event it was traced. Something I wouldn't have to do, if you people would leave me and my family alone."

"One of the officers," Cyrus Krantz said, completely ignoring my barb, "was critically injured in the exchange of gunfire." I realized then why it was his voice sounded strange. He was frustrated. I had never heard Cyrus Krantz sound frustrated before. I was surprised. I have to admit, I thought of him as one of those Energizer bunnies. You know, that he just kept going, and going. . . .

"The perpetrators got away," Dr. Krantz went on. "With Seth."

"Shit!" I yelled. Claire, on Michael's lap, opened her eyes very wide, but I didn't care.

"Can't you people do anything right?"

"It's a little difficult, Jessica," Dr. Krantz said, "when you insist upon playing these childish games with us, claiming you no longer have your psychic powers."

"Don't you go blaming me," I yelled into the phone, "for your incompetence!"

"Jessica," Dr. Krantz said. "Calm down."

"I can't calm down," I shouted. "Not when that kid's still out there. Not when—"

My voice caught. Because, of course, it was all coming back. The fear and terror I'd felt in my dream—my dream about Seth.

Only it hadn't been a dream. Well, to me it had. But it was Seth's reality. A reality that had gone spinning out of control the minute he'd been snatched off his bike in the synagogue parking lot the day before. Who knew what all he'd endured since that moment? All I could see—all I could feel—was what Seth was seeing and experiencing at the exact moment my mind, expansive in sleep, reached out to him.

And that was the cold confinement of the closet he'd been locked into. The throbbing pain of the ropes cutting into his wrists, cruelly tied behind his back. The rough gag biting into the corners of his mouth. The muffled but still terrifying sounds he could hear outside the closet door.

That was Seth Blumenthal's reality. And my nightmare.

The fact that that nightmare was ongoing was almost more than I could bear.

"Jessica," Cyrus Krantz was saying. "I know how you feel about me, and about my organization. But I swear to you, if you would just give us another chance—one more chance for us to work together—you won't regret it. We need to find this boy, Jessica, and soon. He's in danger. Real danger. The people who have him are animals. Anyone who would torture a twelve-year-old—"

"What?" I'd been pacing up and down the hallway with the cordless phone gripped in my hand. Now I froze. "What do you mean, torture?"

"Jessica," Dr. Krantz said. "Haven't you realized by now that all of this—Nate, the synagogue, Seth—is connected?"

"Connected?" Something was buzzing inside my head. "To Seth? Connected how?"

"How do you think the people who set that fire at the synagogue knew where to find the scrolls?" Dr. Krantz asked. "Think about it, Jessica. Who would know exactly where those scrolls were kept? Someone who would have been reading from them on his birthday today."

Seth. Seth Blumenthal.

I couldn't believe it.

He didn't wait for the information to digest. Dr. Krantz said, quickly, "That's why I called. We desperately need your help, Jessica. Listen to me—"

"No, you listen to me," I said. "I tried to do things your way, and all it did was get a cop shot. We're going to do things *my* way now."

Dr. Krantz sounded more frustrated than ever. In fact, now he sounded kind of pissed off. "Oh, yes? And how, precisely, are we going to do that?"

But since of course I had no idea, I couldn't answer his question. Instead, I pressed the Talk button, ending the call.

"Whoa," Mike said, looking at me from over Claire's shoulder. She sat, seemingly frozen, in his lap. "Are you . . . are you okay?"

"No," I said. I lifted a hand to my hair, then noticed that my fingers were shaking. Slowly, I began to slide down the wall, until I was sitting in the middle of the hallway. "No, I'm not all right."

That's when I heard a voice calling from the phone, "Mastriani? Mastriani!"

Like someone in a dream, I brought the receiver to my ear. "Hello?"

"Mastriani, it's me." Rob's voice sounded irritated. "Remember? You put me on hold."

"Rob." I had completely forgotten about him. "Rob. Yeah. Sorry. Look, I can't go out tonight. Something came up."

"Something came up," he repeated, slowly.

"Yes," I said. I felt as if I were underwater. "I'm really sorry. It's Seth. The cops couldn't get to him, and there was a shootout, and now one of them is in critical condition, and those people still have Seth, and I've got to find him before they kill him, too."

"Whoa," Rob said. "Slow down. Who's Seth?"

"Dr. Krantz thinks there's a connection," I said. In some distant part of my brain, I realized I must have sounded to Rob like I was babbling. Maybe I *was* babbling. I just couldn't believe it. A cop. A cop had been shot. And Seth was still out there. Seth was still in danger. "A connection between Nate, Seth, and the synagogue."

"Wait a minute," Rob said. "Dr. Krantz? When did you talk to Krantz? Was that him just now?"

"I'm sorry, Rob," I said. I could see Mickey and Claire looking at me with growing concern. I knew I'd have to pull myself together soon, or Mike would go get my mother. "Look, I've got to go—"

But Rob, as usual, was already taking charge of the situation.

"What's the connection?" Rob wanted to know. "What does Krantz say?"

All I wanted to do was hang up the phone, go upstairs to my room, and climb into bed. Yes, that was it. That was what I needed to do. Go back to sleep, and wake up again tomorrow, so that all of this would just seem like a bad dream.

"Mastriani!" Rob yelled in my ear. "What's the connection?"

"It's the symbol, okay?" I couldn't believe he was yelling at me. I mean, I wasn't the one who'd shot a cop, or anything. "The one that was on Nate's chest. It's the same thing that was spray-painted onto the headstones at the synagogue."

"What does it look like?" Rob wanted to know. "This symbol?"

Look, Rob is my soul mate and all, but that doesn't mean that there aren't times when I don't feel like hauling off and decking him. Now was one of those times.

"Jeez, Rob," I said. "You were there in that cornfield with me, remember?" This caused a pointed look to be exchanged between my brother and his girlfriend, but I ignored them. "Didn't you notice what Nate had on his chest?"

Rob's voice was strangely quiet. "No, not really," he said. "I didn't . . . I didn't actually look. That kind of thing . . . well, I don't really do too well, you know, at the sight of . . ."

Blood. He didn't say it, but then, he didn't have to. All my annoyance with him dissipated. Just like that.

Well, love will do that to you.

"It was this squiggly line," I explained. "With an arrow coming out of one end."

"An arrow," Rob echoed.

"Yeah," I said. "An arrow."

"An M? The squiggly line. Was it shaped like a M, only on its side?"

"I don't know," I said. "I guess so. Look, Rob, I don't feel so good. I gotta go—"

Then Rob said a strange thing. Something that got my attention right away, even though I was feeling so lousy, like I was going to pass out, practically.

He said, "It's not an arrow."

I had been about to press the Talk button and hang up the phone. When he said that, however, I stopped myself. "What do you mean, it's not an arrow?"

"Jess," he said. The fact that he used my first name made me realize the situation was far from normal. "I think I might know who these people are. The people who are doing this stuff."

I didn't even hesitate. It was like all of a sudden, the blood that had seemed frozen in my veins was flowing again.

"I'll meet you at the Stop and Shop," I said. "Come pick me up."

"Mastriani—"

"Just be there," I said, and hung up. Then I threw down the phone, got up, and started for the stairs.

"Jess, wait," Michael called. "Where are you going?"

"Out," I called back. "Tell Mom I'll be home soon."

And then, after struggling into my hat and coat, I was tearing off down the street. I couldn't help noticing as I jogged that while our own driveway was still full of snow, the Thompkinses' driveway had been shoveled so clean, you could practically have played basketball on it. All the snow that had been shoveled away was piled along the curb, as neatly as if a plow had pushed it there.

But it hadn't been the work of a plow. Oh, no. It was the work of a person. Namely, my brother Douglas.

Love. It makes people do the craziest things.

CHAPTER

10

Chick—owner and proprietor of Chick's Bar and Motorcycle Club—looked down at the drawing I had made and went, "Oh, sure. The True Americans."

I looked at the squiggle. It was kind of hard to see in the dark gloom of the bar.

"Are you sure?" I asked. "I mean . . . you really know what this is?"

"Oh, yeah." Chick was eating a meatball sandwich he'd made for himself back in the kitchen. He'd offered one to each of us, as well, but we'd declined the invitation. Our loss, Chick had said.

Now a large piece of meatball escaped from between the buns Chick clutched in one of his enormous hands, and it dropped down onto the drawing I'd made. Chick brushed it away with a set of hairy knuckles.

"Yeah," he said, squinting down at the drawing in the blue-and-red neon light from the Pabst Blue Ribbon sign behind the bar. "Yeah, that's it, all right. They all got it tattooed right here." He indicated the webbing between his thumb and index finger. "Only you got it sideways, or something."

He turned the drawing so that instead of looking like it looked like .

"There," Chick said. There was sauce in his goatee, but he didn't seem to know it . . . or care, anyway. "Yeah. That's how it's supposed to look. See? Like a snake?"

"Don't tread on me," Rob said.

"Don't what?" I asked.

It was weird to be sitting in a bar with Rob. Well, it would have been weird to have been sitting in a bar with anyone, seeing as how I am only sixteen and not actually allowed in bars. But it was particularly weird to be in this bar, and with Rob. It was the same bar Rob had taken me to that first time he'd given me a ride home from detention, nearly a year earlier, back when he hadn't realized I was jailbait. We hadn't imbibed or anything—just burgers and Cokes—but it had been one of the best nights of my entire life.

That was because I had always wanted to go to Chick's, a biker bar I had been passing every year since I was a little kid, whenever I went with my dad to the dump to get rid of our Christmas tree.

Far outside of the city limits, Chick's held mystery for a Townie like me—though Ruth, and most of the rest of the other people I knew, called it a Grit bar, filled as it was with bikers and truckers.

That night, however—even though it was a Saturday—the place was pretty much devoid of customers. That was on account of all the snow. It was no joke, trying to ride a motorcycle through a foot and a half of fresh powder. Rob thankfully hadn't even tried it, and had come to get me instead in his mother's pickup.

But he had been one of the few to brave the mostly unplowed back countryroads. With the exception of Rob and me, Chick's was empty, of both clientele and employees. Neither the bartender nor the fry cook had made it in. Chick hadn't been too happy about having to make his own sandwich. But mostly, if you ask me, because he was so huge, he didn't fit too easily in the small galley kitchen out back.

"Don't tread on me," Rob repeated, for my benefit. "Remember? That was printed on one of the first American flags, along with a coiled snake." He held up my drawing, but tilted it the way Chick had. "That thing on the end isn't an arrow. It's the snake's head. See?"

All I saw was still just a squiggly line with an arrow coming out of it. But I went, "Oh, yeah," so I wouldn't seem too stupid.

"So, these True Americans," I said. "What are they? A motorcycle gang, like the Hell's Angels, or something?"

"Hell, no!" Chick exploded, spraying bits of meatball and bread around. "Ain't a one of 'em could ride his way out of a paper bag!"

"They're a militia group, Mastriani," Rob explained, showing a bit more patience than his friend and mentor, Chick. "Run by a guy who grew up around here . . . Jim Henderson."

"Oh," I said. I was trying to appear worldly and sophisticated and all, since I was in a bar. But it was kind of hard. Especially when I didn't understand half of what anybody was saying. Finally, I gave up.

"Okay," I said, resting my elbows on the sticky, heavily graffitied bar. "What's a militia group?"

Chick rolled his surprisingly pretty blue eyes. They were hard to notice, being mostly hidden from view by a pair of straggly gray eyebrows.

"You know," he said. "One of those survivalist outfits, live way out in the backwoods. Won't pay their taxes, but that don't seem to stop 'em from feeling like they got a right to steal all the water and electricity they can."

"Why won't they pay their taxes?" I asked.

"Because Jim Henderson doesn't approve of the way the government spends his hard-earned money," Rob said. "He doesn't want his taxes going to things like education and welfare . . . unless the right people are the ones receiving the education and welfare."

"The right people?" I looked from Rob to Chick questioningly. "And who are the right people?"

Chick shrugged his broad, leather-jacketed

shoulders. "You know. Your basic blond, blue-eyed, Aryan types."

"But . . ." I fingered the smooth letters of a woman's name—BETTY—that had been carved into the bar beneath my arms. "But the true Americans are the Native Americans, right? I mean, they aren't blond."

"It ain't no use," Chick said, with his mouth full, "arguin' semantics with Jim Henderson. To him, the only true Americans're the ones that climbed down offa the *Mayflower* . . . white Christians. And you ain't gonna tell 'im differently. Not if you don't want a twelve gauge up your hooha."

I raised my eyebrows at this. I wasn't sure what a *hooha* was. I was pretty sure I didn't *want* to know.

"Oh," I said. "So they killed Nate . . ."

". . . because he was black," Rob finished for me.

"And they burned down the synagogue . . ."

". . . because it's not Christian," Rob said.

"So the only true Americans, according to Jim Henderson," I said, "are people who are exactly like . . . Jim Henderson."

Chick finished up his last bite of meatball sandwich. "Give the girl a prize," he said, with a grin, revealing large chunks of meat and bread trapped between his teeth.

I slapped the bar so hard with the flat of my hand, it stung.

"I don't believe this," I yelled, while both Rob and Chick looked at me in astonishment. "Are you saying that all this time, there's been this freaky hate group running around town, and nobody's bothered to do anything about it?"

Rob regarded me calmly. "And what should someone have done, Mastriani?" he asked.

"Arrested them, already!" I yelled.

"Can't arrest a man on account of his beliefs," Chick reminded me. "A man's entitled to believe whatever he wants, no matter how back-ass-ward it might be."

"But he still has to pay his taxes," I pointed out.

"True enough," Chick said. "Only ol' Jim never had two nickels to rub together, so I doubt the county ever thought it'd be worth its while to go after him for tax evasion."

"How about," I said, coldly, "kidnapping and murder? The county might think those worth its while."

"Imagine so," Chick said, looking thoughtful. "Don't know what ol' Jim must be thinking. Isn't like 'im, really. I always thought Jimmy was, you know, all blow and no go."

"Perhaps the arrival," Rob said, "of the Thompkinses, the first African-American family to come to town, offended Mr. Henderson. Aroused in him a feeling of righteous indignation."

Chick stared at Rob, clearly impressed. "Ooh," he said. "Righteous indignation. I'm going to remember that one."

"Right," I said, slipping off my barstool. "Well, that's it, then. Let's go."

Both Chick and Rob blinked at me.

"Go?" Chick echoed. "Where?"

I couldn't believe he even had to ask. "To Jim Henderson's place," I said. "To get Seth Blumenthal."

Chick had been swallowing a sip of beer as I said this. Well, okay, not a sip, exactly. Guys like Chick don't sip, they guzzle.

In any case, when I said this, he let loose what had been in his mouth in a plume that hit Rob, me, and the jukebox.

"Oh, man," Rob said, reaching for some cocktail napkins Chick kept in a pile behind the bar.

"Yeah, Mr. Chick," I said. "Say it, don't spray it."

"Nobody," Chick said, ignoring us, "is going to Jim Henderson's place. Got it? Nobody."

I couldn't believe it.

"Why not?" I demanded. "I mean, we know they did it, right? It's not like they tried to hide it, or anything. They practically hung up a big sign that says 'We Did It.' So let's go over there and make 'em give Seth back."

Chick looked at me for a moment. Then he threw back his head and laughed. A lot.

"Give the kid back," he chortled. "Wheredja get this one, Wilkins? She's a riot."

Rob wasn't laughing. He looked at me sadly.

"What?" I said. "What's so funny?"

"We can't go to Jim Henderson's, Mastriani," Rob said.

I blinked at him. "Why not?"

"Well, for one thing, Henderson shoots at the

water meter-men the county sends out," Rob said. "You think he's not going to try to take us out?"

"Um," I said. "Hello? That's why we sneak in."

"Little lady," Chick said, stubbing a finger thickly encrusted with motorcycle grease at me. I didn't mind him calling me little lady because, well, there wasn't much I could do about it, seeing as how he was about three times as big as me. Mr. Goodhart would have been proud of the progress I was making. Normally the size of my opponent was just about the last thing I considered before tackling someone. "You don't know squat. Didn't I hear you say these folks already shot up a cop earlier today, on account of not wanting to give up some kid they got hold of?"

"Yes," I said. "But the officers involved weren't prepared for what they were up against. We'll be ready."

"Mastriani," Rob said, shaking his head. "I get where you're coming from. I really do. But we aren't talking the Flintstones here. These guys have a pretty sophisticated setup."

"Yeah," Chick said, after letting out a long, aromatic belch. "You're talking some major security precautions. They got the barbed wire, guard dogs, armed sentries—"

"*What?*" I was so mad, I felt like kicking something. "Are you *kidding* me? These guys have all that? And the cops just *let* them?"

"No law against fences and guard dogs,"

Chick said, with a shrug. "And a man's allowed to carry a rifle on his own property—"

"But he's not allowed to shoot cops," I pointed out. "And if what you're saying about these True Americans is accurate, then somebody in that group did just that, earlier today, over at the trailer park by Mr. Shaky's. They got away—with a twelve-year-old hostage. I'm willing to bet they're holed up now with this Jim Henderson guy. And if we don't do something, and soon, that kid is going to end up in a cornfield, same as Nate Thompkins."

Rob and Chick exchanged glances. And in those glances, despite the darkness of the bar, I was able to catch a glimpse of something I didn't like. Something I didn't like at all.

And that was hopelessness.

"Look," I said, my hands going to my hips. "I don't care how secure their fortress is. Seth Blumenthal is in there, and it's up to us to get him out."

Chick shook his head. For the first time, he looked serious . . . serious and sad.

"Little lady," he said. "Jimmy's crazy as they come, but one thing he ain't is stupid. There ain't gonna be a scrap of evidence to connect him with any of this stuff, except the fact that he's head of the group that claimed responsibility. Bustin' in there— which'd be damn near impossible, seeing as how you can't even approach Jim's place by road. It's so far back into the woods, ain't no way the plows can get to it—to rescue some kid is just plain stupid. Ten to one," Chick said, "that boy is long dead."

"No," I said, quietly. "He isn't dead, actually."

Chick looked startled. "Now how in hell," he wanted to know, "could you know that?"

Rob lifted his forehead from his hands, into which he'd sunk it earlier.

"Because," he answered, bleakly. "She's Lightning Girl."

Chick studied me appraisingly in the neon glow. I'm sure my face, like his, must have been an unflattering shade of purple. I probably resembled Violet from that Willy Wonka movie. You know, after she ate the gum.

But Chick must have seen something there that he liked, since he didn't end the conversation then and there.

"You think we should go busting in there," he said, slowly, "and get that kid out?"

"Busting," I said, "is not the word I would use. I think we could probably come up with a more subtle form of entry. But yes. Yes, I do."

"Wait." Rob shook his head. "Wait just a minute here. Mastriani, this is insane. We can't get involved in this. This is a job for the cops—"

"—who don't know what they're up against," I said. "Forget it, Rob. One cop already got shot on account of me. I'm not going to let anyone else get hurt, if I can help it."

"Anyone else," Rob burst out. "What about yourself? Have you ever stopped to think these guys might have a bullet with your name on it next?"

"Rob." I couldn't believe how myopic he was

being. "Jim Henderson isn't going to shoot me."

Rob looked shocked. *"Why not?"*

"Because I'm a girl, of course."

Rob said a very bad word in response to this. Then he pushed away from the bar and went stalking over to the jukebox . . . which he punched. Not hard enough to break it, but hard enough so that Chick looked up and went, "Hey!"

Rob didn't apologize though. Instead, he said, looking at Chick with appeal in his gray eyes, "Can you help me out here? Can you please explain to my girlfriend that she must be suffering from a chemical imbalance if she thinks I'm letting her anywhere near Jim Henderson's place?"

Which was a horribly sexist thing to say, and which I knew I should have resented, but I couldn't, since he'd called me the G word. You know. His *girlfriend*. It was the first time I'd ever heard him call me that. Within earshot of someone else, I mean.

Being his date at that Christmas Eve wedding didn't look so far out of the realm of possibility now.

But Chick, instead of doing as Rob had asked, and telling me to forget about busting in on the True Americans, stroked his goatee thoughtfully. "You know," he said. "It isn't the worst idea I ever heard."

Rob stared at him in horror.

"Hey," Chick said, defensively. "I ain't saying

she should go in alone. But a kid's dead, Wilkins. And if I know Henderson, this other one hasn't got much time left."

I threw Rob a triumphant look, as if to say, *See? I'm not crazy after all.*

"And you might say," Chick went on, "this is a homegrown problem, Wilkins. I mean, Henderson's one of our own. Ain't it appropriate that we be the ones to mete out the justice? I can put in a few calls and have enough boys over here in five minutes, it'd put the National Guard to shame."

I raised my eyebrows, impressed by the *mete out the justice* line.

Rob wasn't going for it, though. "Even if we did agree this was a good idea," he said, "which I am not doing, you said yourself it's inaccessible. There's nearly two feet of snow on the ground. How are we even going to get near the place?"

Chick did a surprising thing, then. He crooked a finger at us, then started walking—though, given his girth and height, lumbering was really more the word for it—toward the back door.

I followed him, with Rob reluctantly trailing behind me. Chick went down a short hallway that opened out into a sort of a ramshackle garage. Wind whistled through the haphazardly thrown up wooden slats that made up the walls.

Flicking on the single electric bulb that served

as a light, Chick strode forward until he came to something covered with a tarp.

"Voilà," he said, in what I assumed was a purposefully bad European accent.

Then he flung back the tarp to reveal two brand-new snowmobiles.

CHAPTER

11

Hey, I'll admit it. I wanted on that snowmobile. I wanted on it, bad.

Can you blame me? I'd never been on one before.

And for someone who likes going fast, well, what's more thrilling than going fast over snow? Oh, sure, I'd been skiing before, over at the dinky slopes of Paoli Peaks. It had been fun and all. For like an hour. I mean, let's face it, Indiana is not exactly known for its mountainous terrain, so the Peaks got old kind of fast for any thrill seeker worthy of the name.

But nothing could compare to the sensation of zipping over all that thickly packed white stuff with my arms wrapped tightly around the waist of my hot, if disapproving, boyfriend.

Oh, it was good. It was real good.

But I have to admit, the part after we'd pulled

up in front of the True Americans' barbed-wire fence, and just sat there with the engine switched off, gazing at the lights of Jim Henderson's house, glimmering through the trees?

Yeah, that part wasn't so fun.

That was on account of the fact that deep in the backwoods of Indiana, on a late November evening, it is very, very cold. Bone-chillingly cold. Mind-numbingly cold. Or at least toe and finger-numbingly cold.

You would think that Rob and I could have thought up something to do, you know, to pass the time—as well as keep warm—while we waited for Chick to catch up to us with the backup he'd promised. But given the fact that Rob was still so mad we were here at all, there hadn't been much, you know, of *that* going on. In fact, none at all.

"So what are we waiting for, again?" I asked.

"Reinforcements," was Rob's terse reply.

"Yeah," I said. "I get that part. But can't we just, you know, go and wait inside?"

"And what are we going to do," Rob said, "if we find Seth?"

"Bust on out of there," I said.

"Using what as a weapon?"

I thought a minute. "Our rapier wit?"

"Like I said."

Well. So much for that.

Rob didn't seem as cold as I was. Why is that? How come boys never get as cold as girls do? And also, what's with the peeing thing? Like how come I totally had to pee, and he didn't? He'd had as many Cokes back at Chick's as I did.

And even if he had had to pee, it wouldn't have been any big deal for him. I mean, he could have just gone over to any old tree and done it.

But for me, it would have been like this major production. And a lot more of me would have been exposed to the forces of nature. Which, with it being like ten below, or something, were pretty harsh.

Whatever. Life is just unfair. That's all I have to say.

Not that I had it so bad, I guess. I mean, comparatively, I guess I've always had it pretty good. I mean, my parents are still together, and seem pretty happy to stay that way . . . except, you know, when one of us kids is causing them trouble, like hearing voices that aren't there, or dropping out of Harvard, or being struck by lightning and getting psychic powers and then causing the family restaurant to be burned down.

You know. The usual parental stresses.

At least we were pretty well off. I mean, no one was buying me my own pony—or Harley—but we weren't exactly on welfare, either. In all, the Mastriani family had it pretty good.

As opposed to, just for an example, the Wilkins family. I mean, Rob had been working in his uncle's garage pretty much full time since he was like fourteen or something, just to help his mom make ends meet. He hadn't seen his dad since he was a little kid. He didn't even know where his dad was.

But I did. I knew where Rob's dad was.

Not that I was very grateful for the information. But there it was, embedded in my brain just like Seth Blumenthal's current location and status.

The question was, should I tell Rob, or not?

Would I want to know? I mean, if my dad had disappeared when I was a little kid. Had just walked out on Mom and Mike and Douglas and me. Would I want to know where he was now? Would I even care?

Yeah. Probably. If only so I could go pound his face in.

But would Rob want to know?

There was only one way, really, to find out. But I really, really didn't want to do it. Just come out and ask him if he wanted to know, I mean. Because I didn't want him to know I'd been snooping. I hadn't, really. His mom had needed that apron from her room. Was it my fault that while I'd been in there, I'd happened to see a picture of Rob's dad? And that afterward, as always tended to happen when I saw photos of missing people, I dreamed about his dad, and exactly where he was now? Was it my fault that, thanks to that stupid lightning, that I can't see a picture—or sometimes, even smell the sweater or pillow—of a missing person without getting a mental picture of their exact location?

"Listen," I said, pressing myself a little harder against his back. It was damned cold on the back of that snowmobile. "Rob, I—"

"Mastriani," Rob said, sounding tired. "Not now, okay?"

"What?" I asked, defensively. "I was just going to—"

"I am not going to tell you," Rob said.

"Tell me what?"

"What I'm on probation for. Okay? You can forget it. Because you're never getting it out of me. You can drag me out to the middle of nowhere," he said, "on some lunatic mission to stop a murdering white supremacist. You can make me sit for hours in sub-zero temperatures until my fingers feel like they are going to fall off. You can even tell me that you love me. But I am not going to tell you why I got arrested."

I digested this. While this was not, of course, the subject I'd meant to bring up, it was nonetheless a very interesting one. Perhaps more interesting, even, than the current location of Rob's father. To me, anyway.

"I didn't tell you that I love you," I said, after some thought, "because I wanted you to tell me what you're on probation for. Although I do want to know. I told you that I love you because—"

Rob swung around on the back of the snowmobile and threw a gloved hand over my mouth. "Don't," he said. His light-colored eyes were easy to distinguish in the moonlight. Because yeah, there was a moon. A pretty full one, too, hanging low in the cold, cloudless sky. Any other time, it might have been romantic. If, you know, it hadn't been like twenty below, and I hadn't had to pee, and my boyfriend had actually sort of liked me.

"Don't start on that again," Rob said, keeping his hand over my mouth. "Remember what happened last time."

"I liked what happened last time," I said, from behind his fingers.

"Yeah," Rob said. "Well, so did I. Too much, okay? So just keep your I love yous to yourself, all right, Mastriani?"

Sure. Like that was going to happen, after a girl hears a thing like that.

"Rob," I said, tightening my arms around his waist. "I—"

But I never got to finish. That was on account of a figure moving toward us through the trees. We heard the snow crunching beneath his feet.

Rob said a bad word and turned on the flashlight Chick had loaned us.

"Who's there?" he hissed, and shined the flashlight full on into the face of none other than Cyrus Krantz.

Now it was my turn to say a bad word.

"Shhh," Dr. Krantz said. "Jessica, please!"

"Well, whatever," I said, disgustedly. "What are you doing here?"

I couldn't believe his getup. Dr. Krantz's, I mean. He looked like somebody out of *Icestation Zebra.* He had the full-on arctic gear, complete with puffy camouflage ski pants. I had barely recognized him with all the fur trim on his hood.

"I followed you, of course," Dr. Krantz replied. "Is this where they're holding Seth, Jessica?"

"Would you get out of here?" I couldn't tell which was making me madder, the fact that he was putting our plan to rescue Seth in jeopardy, or that he'd interrupted Rob and me just when things had been starting to get interesting. "You're going to ruin everything. How did you get out here, anyway?" If he said snowmobile, I was going to seriously reconsider my refusal to work for him. Any institution that willingly supplied its employees with snowmobiles was one I could see myself getting behind.

"Never mind about that," Dr. Krantz said. "Really, Jessica, this is just too ridiculous. You shouldn't be here. You're going to get hurt."

"*I'm* going to get hurt?" I laughed bitterly— though quietly. "Sorry, Doc, but I think you got it backward. So far the only person who's gotten hurt is one of yours."

"And Nate Thompkins," Dr. Krantz reminded me softly. "Don't forget him."

As if I could. As if he wasn't half the reason I was out there, freezing my *hooha* off. I hadn't forgotten my promise to myself to try to help Tasha, if I could. And the best way to help her, I couldn't help thinking, was to bring her brother's murderers to justice.

And of course to keep them from hurting anybody else. Such as Seth Blumenthal.

"Nobody's forgetting about Nate," I whispered. "We're just going to take care of this in our own way, all right? Now get out of here, before you mess everything up."

"Jessica," Dr. Krantz said. "Rob. I really must object. If Seth Blumenthal is being harbored on this property, you are under an obligation to report it, then stand back and allow the appropriate law enforcement agents to do their—"

"Oh, bite me," I said.

I couldn't be sure, given the way the moonlight, reflecting off all the snow, made it hard to see past the thick lenses of his glasses, but I thought Dr. Krantz blinked a few times.

"I b-beg your pardon," he stammered.

"You heard me," I said. "You and the appropriate law enforcement agents don't have the slightest clue what you're dealing with here, okay?"

"Oh." Now Dr. Krantz sounded sarcastic, which was sort of amusing, considering the fact that he was such a geek. "And I suppose you do."

"Better than you," I said. "At least we've got a chance at infiltrating them from the inside, instead of going in there blasting away, and possibly getting Seth killed in the crossfire."

"Infiltration?" Dr. Krantz sounded appalled. "What are you talking about? You can't possibly think you have a better chance at—"

"Oh, yeah?" I narrowed my eyes at him. "What number comes after nine?"

He looked at me like I was crazy. "What? What does that have to do with—"

"Just answer the question, Dr. Krantz," I said. "What number comes after nine?"

"Why, ten, of course."

"Wrong," I said. "What are Coke cans made out of?"

"Aluminum, of course. Jessica, I—"

"Wrong again," I said. "The answer to both questions, Dr. Krantz, is tin. I've just administered a Grit test, and you failed miserably. There is no way you are going to be able to pass for a local. Now get out of here, before you ruin it for the rest of us."

"This," Dr. Krantz said, looking scandalized, "is ridiculous. Rob, surely you—"

But Rob straightened on the back of the snowmobile, his head turned in the direction of the lights from Jim Henderson's house.

"Bogey," he said, "at twelve o'clock. Krantz, if you don't get the hell out of sight, you're gonna find yourself with a belly full of buckshot."

"W-what?" Dr. Krantz looked around nervously. "What are you—"

Rob was off the snowmobile and shoving Cyrus Krantz behind a tree before the good doctor knew what was happening. At the same time, I saw what Rob had seen, a light coming toward us through the thick trees on Jim Henderson's side of the barbed wire. As the light came closer, I saw that it came from one of those old-fashioned kerosene lanterns. The lantern was held by a big man in red-plaid hunting gear, a rifle in his other hand, and a dog big enough to pass for a small pony at his side.

The dog, when it noticed us, began hurtling through the snow in our direction. For a second or two, as it came careening toward us, its long tongue lolling and its eyes blazing, I thought it was one of those hell dogs. . . . You know, from that *Hound of the Baskervilles* they made us read in ninth grade?

But as it got closer, I realized it was just your run of the mill German shepherd. You know, the kind that clamp down on your throat and won't let go, even if you hit them over the head with a socket wrench.

Fortunately, just as this particular German shepherd was preparing to leap over the barbed wire between us and do just that, the guy with the rifle went, "Chigger! Down!" and the dog collapsed into the snow not two feet away from Rob and me, growling menacingly, with its gaze never wavering from us.

The man with the rifle put the lantern down, reached into his pocket, and pulled something out. *Handgun,* I thought, my heart thudding so loudly in my chest, I thought it might cause an avalanche. If there'd been any cliffs around, anyway. *The rifle's too messy. He's going to put a bullet through each of our skulls and let Chigger eat our frozen carcasses.*

Sometimes it really did seem like the whole world was conspiring against me ever seeing Rob in a tux.

"Hey," Rob said, keeping his hands in the air and his gaze on Chigger. "Hey, don't shoot. We don't mean any harm. We just want to talk to Jim."

But it turned out the thing Chigger's owner

had taken out of his pocket wasn't a gun. It was a Walkie-Talkie.

"Blue Leader, this is Red Leader," Red Plaid Jacket said into the Walkie-Talkie. "We got intruders over by the south fence. Repeat. Intruders by the south fence."

"We aren't intruders," I said. Then, remembering what our cover story was supposed to be— except of course that we weren't supposed to have let ourselves get caught until *after* Chick and his friends were safely hidden in the bushes and trees around the compound, ready to bust us on out as soon as we successfully found Seth—I quickly amended that claim. "I mean, we *ain't* intruders. We want to join you. We want to be True Americans, too."

Static burst over Red Plaid Jacket's Walkie-Talkie. Apparently, someone was replying to his intruder warning. He must have been speaking in code, though, because I couldn't understand what he was saying.

"Copy that, Red Leader," the voice said. "Tag and transport. Repeat, tag and transport."

Red Plaid Jacket put his Walkie-Talkie away, then signaled for Rob and me to climb over the barbed wire. The way he signaled this was, he pointed the rifle at us, and went, "Git on over here."

Climbing over barbed wire is never a pleasant experience. But it is an even less pleasant experience when you are doing it under the watchful gaze of a massive German shepherd named Chigger. Rob went first, and didn't seem to snag anything too vital while climbing. He very politely held as much of the barbed wire down for me as he was able, so that I could arrive uninjured on the other side, as well. I didn't succeed as nimbly as he had, being about a foot shorter than he was, but all that really suffered was the inside seam of my jeans.

Once we were safely on the True Americans' side of the fence, Red Plaid Jacket went, "Git on, then," and signaled, again with the mouth of his rifle, that we should start walking toward the house.

Rob looked back at the snowmobile.

"What about our ride?" he asked. "Is it safe to leave it there?"

Red Plaid Jacket let out a harsh laugh. That wasn't all he let out, either. He also let out a stream of tobacco juice from between his cheek and gum. It landed, in a steaming brown puddle, in the snow.

"Safe from what?" he wanted to know. "The coons? Or the possums?"

This was a comforting response, as it indicated that Red Plaid was as unaware of the presence of Dr. Krantz, hidden behind the thick pines, as he was of the many patrons of Chick's who had answered the call to arms by the owner of their favorite carousing spot . . . or who at least I was hoping would answer that call. And show up soon.

"Move," Red Plaid said to Rob and me.

And so we moved.

CHAPTER

12

It would be wrong to say I enjoyed our long walk toward Jim Henderson's house. I relished any time I got to spend in the presence of Rob Wilkins, as our meetings, now that he had graduated but I remained trapped behind in high school hell, had grown all too infrequent.

No matter how nice the company one might be with, however, it is never pleasant to have a rifle pointed at one's back. While I didn't think Red Plaid Jacket would fire at us in cold blood, there was always the chance that he might trip over Chigger or a stump hidden in the snow, and accidentally pull the trigger.

And though this would solve my problem of how I was going to get Rob to invite me to a formal affair like his uncle's wedding (so I could impress him by now nice I look in a dress), it would not solve it in the right way. So it was with some trepidation that I made the long journey from the south fence to the heart of the True Americans' compound.

Once we got moving, though, I did start to feel a little less cold. Now that the blizzard had blown away, the sky was completely clear, and this far out from the lights of town, it was magically dusted with stars. I could even make out the Milky Way. It might almost have been romantic, a moonlit walk through the freshly fallen snow, the smell of wood smoke hanging tantalizingly in the air.

Except, of course, for the rifle. Oh, and the dangerous German shepherd slogging along beside us.

I am not afraid of dogs, and in general, they seem to like me. So during our walk, since we didn't dare talk to pass the time, I concentrated on trying to get Chigger to give up on the idea of tearing my throat out. I did this by thrusting my hand, whenever Red Plaid Jacket wasn't looking, and the dog came close enough, in front of Chigger's nose. Dogs operate by smell, and I figured if Chigger smelled that I really wasn't the lunchmeat type, he might hesitate about eating me.

Chigger, however, like most males I've encountered in my life, seemed remarkably uninterested in me. Maybe I should have taken Ruth's advice and invested in some perfume, instead of just splashing on some of Mike's Old English Leather now and then.

As we got closer to the buildings we were approaching, I have to admit, I wasn't too impressed. I mean, compared to Jim Henderson's place, David Koresh's compound over in Waco had looked like the freaking Taj Mahal. Henderson's entire operation seemed to consist of nothing more than a ranch-style house, a few trailers, and one rambling barn. Sure, the whole thing had that army barracks, ready-to-mobilize-at-any-minute kind of lack of permanency.

But hello, where was the bathroom? That was all I wanted to know.

To my dismay, Red Plaid Jacket, tailed by the ever faithful Chigger, led us not toward the ranch house, or either of the trailers, but directly to the barn. My chances of finding a working toilet were beginning to look dimmer than ever.

You can imagine my delight then when Red Plaid threw back the massive barn door to reveal what appeared to be the True Americans' command center, or bunker, if you will. Oh, it was no NORAD, don't get me wrong. There were no computers. There wasn't even a TV in sight.

Instead, the seat of Jim Henderson's white supremacist group resembled photos we'd seen in World Civ of Nazi headquarters, back in the forties. There were a lot of long tables, at which sat a good many fair-haired gentlemen. (Apparently, we had interrupted their supper.) And there was a giant flag hanging against the back wall. But instead of a swastika, the flag depicted the symbol that had been carved into Nate Thompkins's chest, and spray-painted onto the overpass and on the overturned headstones at the Jewish cemetery. It was the coiled snake Chick had described, with the words DON'T TREAD ON ME beneath it.

But may I just point out that there the resemblance to the Nazi war machine ended? Because the gentlemen, fair-haired as they were, gathered in the large, drafty room, were neither as tidily dressed nor as intelligent looking as your average 1940s-style Nazi, and seemed also to prefer body art to actual hygiene, a choice perhaps thrust upon them by the lack of easily available running water, if what Chick had said about Jim Henderson refusing to pay his water bill was true.

There weren't only men gathered in Henderson's barn, however. Oh, no. There were women, too, and even children. I mean, who else was going to serve the men their food? And a fine, healthy lot those women and children looked, too. The women's garb I instantly recognized as typical of a local religious sect which, besides favoring snake-handling and coming-to-the-water-to-be-born-again, also forbade its female practitioners from cutting their hair or wearing pants. This made it difficult for girls belonging to this religious group to participate in physical education classes in the public school system, as it is almost impossible to climb a rope or learn the breast stroke in a dress, so many of them opted for homeschooling.

The children were a pasty-faced, runny-nosed

lot, who seemed as uninterested in a man with a rifle dragging two perfect strangers into their midst as I would have been by cooking lessons from Great-aunt Rose.

"Jimmy," Red Plaid Jacket said, to a sandy-haired man at the head of one of the long tables, who'd just been presented with a plate of what looked to me—considering that I hadn't eaten since downing a turkey sandwich around noon—like delectable fried chicken. "These're the kids we found sneakin' around by the south fence."

Kids! I resented the implication on Rob's behalf. I of course am used to being mistaken for a child, given my relatively diminutive size. But Rob stood a good twelve inches taller than me. . . .

And, I soon noticed, twelve inches taller than the leader of the True Americans, that fine, upstanding citizen who had, if we weren't mistaken, killed one kid, abducted another, attempted to murder a law enforcement officer, and burned down a synagogue.

That's right. Jim Henderson was short.

Really, really short. Like Napoleon short. Like Danny Devito short.

He also seemed kind of miffed that we had interrupted his dinner.

"What the hell you want?" Henderson inquired, showing some of those exemplary leadership qualities for which he was apparently so deeply admired by his followers.

I looked at Rob. He appeared to be at a loss for words. Either that or he was doing one of those

Native American-silence things, to psych out our captors. Rob reads a lot of books that take place on Indian reservations.

I felt it was up to me to salvage the situation. I went, "Gee, Mr. Henderson, it's a real honor to meet you. Me and Hank here, well, we just been admirers of yours for so long."

Henderson sucked on his fried-chickeny fingers, his sandy-colored eyebrows raised. "That so?" he said.

"Yes," I said. "And when we saw what ya'll did to that, um, Jew church, we decided we had to come up and offer our, um, congratulations. Hank and me, we think we'd make real good True Americans, because we both hate blacks and Jews, and stuff."

There appeared to be a good deal more interest in Rob and me now that I had begun speaking. Nearly everyone in the barn was looking at us, in sort of stunned silence. Everyone except Chigger, I mean. Chigger had found a plate of chicken bones, and was consuming them with great noise and rapidity. I noticed no one leapt to stop him, which proved that the True Americans were not only despicable human beings, but also lousy pet owners, as everyone knows you should never let a dog eat chicken bones.

Henderson was looking at us with more interest than anyone. Unlike Chigger, he seemed completely oblivious to the chicken on his plate. He went, "Why?"

I'd been prepared for this question. I said,

"Well, you should take us because Hank here, he is really good with his hands. He's a mechanic, you know, and he can fix just about anything. So if you ever got a tank, or whatever, and it broke down, well, Hank'd be your man. And me, well, I may not look like it, but I'm pretty swift on my feet. In a fight, you wouldn't want me on your bad side, let me tell you."

Henderson looked bored. He leaned forward to pick a piece of chicken off the bone and pop it into his little mouth. He reminded me, as he did it, of a baby bird. Except that he had a sandy-colored mustache.

"That ain't what I mean," he said. "I mean, why do you hate the blacks and Jews?"

"Oh." This was not a question I'd been prepared for. I hurried to think of a reply. "Because as everyone knows," I said, "the Jews, they made up that whole Holocaust thing, you know, so they could get their hands on Israel. And black people, well, they're taking away all our jobs."

This was not apparently the correct answer, since Jim looked away from me. Instead, he stared at Rob. He appeared to be sizing up my boyfriend. I had seen this kind of appraising look before. It was the kind of look that little guys always gave to big guys, right before they barreled their tiny heads into the bigger guy's stomach.

"What about you?" Henderson asked Rob. "Or do you let your woman do your talking for you?"

This caused a ripple of amusement amongst

the men at the dinner tables. Even the women, poised at their husbands' elbows with pitchers of what looked to me like iced tea, seemed to find this hilarious, instead of the piece of sexist crap it was.

Rob, I knew, was being tested. I had not passed the test. That much was clear. It was clear by the fact that Red Plaid Jacket still had his rifle trained on us, just waiting for the order from his boss to blow our heads off. Chigger, I was certain, would gladly lick up whatever mess our scattered brains made upon the barn floor.

It was up to Rob to save us. It was up to Rob to convince Henderson that we were a pair of budding white supremacists.

And I didn't have much faith Rob was going to perform any better than I had. After all, Rob hadn't liked this idea in the first place. He had objected strenuously to it from the start. All he wanted to do, I was sure, was book on out of there, and if it was without Seth, well, that was just too bad. Just so long as we still had heads on our shoulders, I had a feeling Rob would be happy.

So you can imagine my surprise when Rob opened his mouth and this is what came out of it:

"To be born white," he said, "is an honor and a privilege. It is time that all white men and women join together to protect this bond they share by their blood and faith. The responsibility of every American is to protect the welfare of *ourselves*—not those in Mexico, Vietnam, Afghanistan, or some other third-world country. It is time to take America back from drug-addicted welfare recipients living in large urban areas. . . ."

Whoa. If Rob had my attention with this stuff, you can bet he had Jim Henderson's attention—not to mention the rest of the True Americans. You could have heard a pin drop, everybody was listening so intently.

"It's time," Rob went on, "to protect our borders from illegal aliens, and stop the insidious repeal of miscegenation laws and statutes. We need to do away with affirmative action and same-sex marriages. We need to prevent American industry and property from slipping into the hands of the Japanese, Arabs, and Jews. America should be owned by Americans—"

Applause burst from one of the tables at this. It was soon joined by standing ovations from several other tables. In the thunderous cheering that followed, I stared at my boyfriend with total disbelief. Where on earth, I wondered, had he gotten all that stuff? Was there something about Rob I didn't know? I had never heard him say any of that kind of stuff before. Was Claire right? Were all Grits the same?

The applause was cut off abruptly as Jim Henderson climbed to his feet. All eyes were on the tiny figure, really no taller than I was, as he eyed Rob, one finger thoughtfully stroking his thick mustache. Again, the room was silent, except for Chigger, who was enthusiastically licking a now empty plate.

Staring at Rob with a pair of eyes so blue, they almost seemed to blaze, Henderson finally thrust an index finger at him and commanded, "Get . . . that . . . boy . . . some . . . chicken!"

Cheers erupted as one of the women hurried forward to present Rob with a plate of fried chicken. I couldn't believe it. Chicken. They were giving Rob chicken! Easy as that, he'd been accepted into the bosom of the True Americans.

Or was it possible that they knew something I didn't? Like that Rob was maybe already a member?

Hey, I know it was a disloyal thought. And I didn't believe it. Not really. Except that . . . well, it was kind of weird that he'd known exactly the right thing to say to get these freaks to believe we were on their side. And knowing what I did about his dad, it wasn't much of a stretch to imagine there might be a few things Rob hadn't told me . . . and I didn't just mean what he was on probation for.

Rob stood there, smiling shyly as he was applauded. I couldn't help it. I *had* to know. So I asked him, out of the corner of my mouth, "Where'd you come up with that horse shit?"

Rob replied, from the corner of his own mouth, "Public access cable. Would you get this chicken away from me before I barf?"

I grabbed the plate just as Rob was engulfed in a crowd of happy white supremacists, who slapped him on the back and offered him chews from their bags of tobacco. I stood there like an idiot watching him, the plate of chicken getting cold in my hands. I couldn't believe how stupid I'd been. Of *course* Rob wasn't one of them.

But it was scary how easily I'd been swayed into thinking he might have been. Prejudice runs deep. Grits and Townies, blacks and whites . . . you grow up hearing one thing, it's hard to believe that something else might actually be true.

Hard to believe, maybe. But not impossible. I mean, look at Rob. He was nothing like your stereotypical Grit, gleefully chowing down on fried chicken while discussing the supremacy of the white race. Rob didn't even *like* fried chicken.

Who knows how long I would have stood there, admiring the genius of my boyfriend, if a voice at my elbow hadn't gone, "Well, just don't there stand there, girlie. Give that chicken to one of the men and then git on back to the kitchen fer more."

I turned and saw a doughy-faced woman with a kerchief holding back her long blonde hair glaring at me.

"Go on," the woman said, giving me a push toward one of the men's tables. "Git."

I got. I put the chicken down in front of the first man I saw—a gentleman who did not appear to have as many teeth as he did tattoos—then followed Kerchief-Head out a side door. . . .

Into the cold night air.

"Come on," the woman barked at me, when I froze in my tracks, shocked by the sudden cold. "We gotta git the mashed potatoes."

I followed her, thinking, *Well, at least this way, I'll have a chance to look for Seth.* I knew he was here on the compound somewhere. I knew that he was no longer tied up or gagged, but locked into a small, wood-paneled room. That didn't mean he wasn't still scared, though. I could feel his fear around me like a second coat.

Kerchief-Head threw open the door to the ranch house. This, apparently, was where all the cooking was done. I could tell by the intoxicating odors that hit me as I came through the door. Chicken, potatoes, bread . . . it was a dizzying set of aromas for a girl as hungry as I was.

But when we got into the kitchen—which was crowded with other doughy-faced, long-haired women—and I tried to bogart a roll, Kerchief-Head slapped my hands.

"We don't eat," she said, harshly, "until the men're done!"

Whoa, I wanted to say. *Nice operation you got going here. If you're a guy.* What is it with women like Kerchief-Head? I mean, why are they so willing to put up with that kind of treatment? I would way rather have no guy than some guy who tried to make me wait to eat until after he was done.

But I didn't want to blow things with the True Americans, so I dropped the roll like a good white supremacist housewife and asked, "You got a bathroom around here?"

Kerchief-Head pointed down a hallway, but she didn't look too happy about it. I guess she thought I was trying to shirk kitchen duty or something.

I'll tell you something, those True Americans were pretty scary. Even their bathrooms were filled with racist propaganda. I couldn't believe it. Instead of issues of *National Geographic* or *Time* magazine, like in a normal house, there was a copy of *Mein Kampf* to peruse while you were otherwise indisposed. Like these guys had totally missed the part where Hitler turned out to be a maniac or something.

When I was through in the bathroom, I looked up and down the hall to make sure Kerchief-Head or any of her cronies weren't lurking around. Then I started testing doorknobs. I figured when I got to a locked one, that's the one I'd find Seth behind.

It didn't take me long. It wasn't like the house was so big, or anything. The room they were keeping Seth in was way at the end of the hall, past the homeschooling room—instead of the old red, white, and blue, there was another one of those "Don't Tread On Me" flags hanging in there. The door was locked, but it was one of those cheap button locks you only have to turn from the right side to undo. I turned it, opened the door, and looked inside.

Seth Blumenthal, tears streaming down his face, sat up in bed, and blinked at me in the semi-darkness.

"Wh-who are you?" Seth asked, hesitantly. "Wh-what do you want?"

How else was I supposed to reply? The words were out of my mouth before I could stop them. I mean, I'd only seen the movie like seventeen times.

"I'm Luke Skywalker," I said. "I'm here to rescue you."

CHAPTER

13

Seth didn't fall for the Luke Skywalker line. This was one kid you obviously couldn't pull anything over on.

"No," he said. "Who are you, really? You don't look like one of them."

I closed the door behind me, in case Kerchief-Head came looking for me. There was no light in the room, except the moonlight that came filtering in between the wooden boards that covered the windows—always a Martha Stewart "do," boarding up your windows, by the way.

"My name's Jess," I said, to Seth. "And we're going to get you out of here." But not through those windows, I now realized. "Are you hurt anywhere? Can you run?"

"I'm okay," Seth said. "Just my hand."

He held out his right hand. It wasn't hard to see, even in the moonlight, what was wrong with it. Somebody had burned a shape into it, between Seth's thumb and forefinger. The burn was red and blistered. And it was in the shape of a coiled snake.

Just like the shape that had been carved into Nate Thompkins's naked chest.

I knew now how they'd gotten Seth to tell them where to find the Torah.

And I wanted to kill them for it.

First things first, however.

"Six weeks hydro-therapy," I said to him, "that puppy'll be gone. Won't even leave a scar." I knew from my own third-degree burn, which had been roughly the same size, but which I'd received from a motorcycle exhaust pipe when I'd been around his own age. "Okay?"

Seth nodded. He wasn't crying anymore. "That policeman," he said. "The one they shot, back at the trailer. Is he okay?"

"He sure is," I lied. "Now listen, I've got to get back to the kitchen before they notice I'm missing. But I promise I'll be back for you just as soon as the shooting starts."

"Shooting?" Seth looked concerned. "Who's going to start shooting?"

"Friends of mine," I said. "They got the place surrounded." I hoped. "So you just hang in there, and I'll be back for you lickety-split. Got it?"

"I got it," Seth said. Then, as I started for the door, he went, "Hey, Jess?"

I turned. "Yeah?"

"What day is it?"

I told him. He nodded thoughtfully. "Today's my birthday," he said, seemingly to no one in particular. "I'm thirteen."

"Happy birthday," I said. Well, what else was I supposed to say?

I was just sauntering away from the newly relocked door when Kerchief-Head appeared.

"Where do you think you're going?" she demanded. One thing I had to say for the wives of the True Americans, they weren't very polite.

"Oh," I said, giving my ditziest giggle. "I got lost."

Kerchief-Head just glared at me. Then she thrust a huge bowl of something white and glutinous in my arms. Looking down, I realized it was mashed potatoes. Only the True Americans, unlike my dad, hadn't put any garlic in them, so the aroma they gave off was somewhat nondescript.

"Take this to the men," Kerchief-Head said.

"Can do," I told her, and headed out the door.

The big question, of course, was would it work. I mean, would Chick and his friends show up in time for us to get Seth out? And what about Dr. Krantz? Let's not forget about him. The Feds had a major tendency to mess things like surprise attacks up, big time. Would Chick be able to get around whatever idiot scheme Dr. Krantz was probably, at this very moment, cooking up?

I hoped so. Not for my own sake. I didn't much care what happened to me. It was Seth I was worried about. We had to get Seth out.

Oh, yeah. And kill every True American we possibly could.

I don't normally go around wanting to kill people, but when I'd seen that burn on Seth's hand, I'd felt something I'd never felt before. I am no stranger to rage, either. I get mad fast, and I get mad often. But I could never remember feeling the way I had when I'd seen that burn.

I'd felt like killing someone. Really killing them. Not breaking someone's nose, or kicking someone in the groin. I wanted him to pay for branding that kid, and I wanted him to pay with his life.

And I had a pretty good idea who that someone was.

When I got back into the barn, everyone had calmed down from Rob's little speech, and was busy chowing down again. Being the mashed potato girl, I was pretty popular. Guys kept on raising up their plates as I passed, holding them out for me to glop mashed potatoes onto. I obliged, since what else was I supposed to do? I got through it by pretending I was a prison guard, and all these guys were demented serial killers that I was mandated by the state to keep fed.

In the back of my mind, however, this mantra was playing over and over. It went, *Hurry up, Chick. Hurry up, Chick. Hurry up, Chick. Hurry up, Chick.*

When I reached Rob, I saw that he and Henderson were already well on their way to becoming best friends. Well, and why not? Rob would be a boon to any hate group. He was good-looking, great with his hands, and—though I hadn't been aware of this talent until very recently—he was obviously a passionate and lucid orator. I had a feeling that, given enough time, Rob would have been appointed Jim Henderson's right-hand man.

Too bad for the True Americans that it was all an act.

A good one, though. Claire Lippman would have been astounded by Rob's theatrical flair. As I leaned over his chair to lump potatoes onto his plate, he didn't even seem to notice me, he was so wound up in what he was saying . . . something about how the criminals in Washington were selling us out with something called GATT.

Wow. Rob had obviously been watching a lot more CNN than I had.

After piling some potatoes onto Jim Henderson's plate—only for a second did I fantasize about pretending to accidentally drop them into his lap—I moved on to the rest of the table, trying not to notice as I did so a disturbing thing. There were lots of disturbing things to notice in that barn, but the one that I kept coming back to was the men's hands. Each and every one of them had the same tattoo on the webbing between the thumb and forefinger of their right hand. And that was the coiled snake of the "Don't Tread On Me" flag. The same snake that had been on Nate's chest. The same snake that had been burned into Seth's hand. This was some fraternity, let me tell you.

It wasn't until my bowl was almost empty that I felt the cold, wet nudge on one hand. I looked down and saw Chigger, his big brown eyes rolling up at me appealingly. Gone was the menacing growl and raised back hairs. I had food, and Chigger wanted food. Therefore, if I gave Chigger food, I would be Chigger's friend.

I let Chigger lick what remained in the bowl.

I fully intended to go back to the ranch house kitchen and refill that bowl without rinsing it out first. In fact, I was headed toward the barn door to do just that when I noticed something that I didn't like . . . that I didn't like at all. And that was Kerchief-Head, over at Jim Henderson's table, leaning down to whisper something in his ear. As she whispered I saw Jim glance around the room, until at last his gaze found me. Those piercing blue eyes stayed on me, too, until Kerchief-Head finished whatever it was she'd had to say and straightened up.

Look, it could have been a lot of things. It could have been the thing with the roll. Heck, she could have seen me letting Chigger lick the bowl.

But I'm not stupid. I knew what it was. I knew what it was the minute Jim Henderson's gaze landed on me.

Kerchief-Head had told him about catching me in the hallway near where they were keeping Seth. That was all.

We were dead.

It took a little while for it to happen, though. Henderson whispered something back to Kerchief-Head, and she scuttled out of there like a water bug. For a little while, I thought maybe we were all right. You know, that maybe I'd made a mistake. Rob was going on about abominations of nature and how America would never be restored to the great nation it had once been until all Christians banded together, and Henderson seemed to be listening to him pretty intently.

But then I saw something that made my heart stop.

And that was Red Plaid Jacket with the end of his rifle pointed at the back of Seth Blumenthal's neck as he forced the boy to walk across the barn floor, right up to where Jim Henderson and Rob sat.

Everyone stopped talking when they saw this, and once again, the silence in the barn was overwhelming. The only sound I could hear was the sound of Seth's sobs. He had started crying again. I saw him look frantically around the barn, and I knew he was looking for me. Fortunately, I was far enough in the shadows that he hadn't been able to see me, or without a doubt, I'd have been dead.

If I'd known, of course, what was going to happen a minute later anyway, I probably wouldn't have cared so much. As it was, I was actually relieved Seth hadn't spotted me. I sunk my fingers into Chigger's soft fur and willed my heart to start beating again. *Hurry up, Chick. Hurry up, Chick. Hurry up, Chick!*

"Americans," Jim Henderson said to the assembled masses. I could see at once that he was every bit the orator Rob was. Everyone looked at him with that glazed expression of adoration I recognized from that movie about the Jim Jones massacre. Henderson was these people's messiah on earth.

"We've made some fine new friends tonight," Henderson went on, slapping a hand to Rob's shoulder. The only reason he'd been able to reach it was that Rob was sitting and he was standing. "And I for one am grateful. Grateful that Hank and Ginger found their way to our little flock."

Ginger? Who the hell was Ginger? Then, as a good many heads turned in my direction, I realized Rob had told them my name was Ginger.

He is such a card.

"But however impressed we may be by Hank and Ginger's professed dedication to our cause," Henderson went on, "there's really only one way to test the loyalty of a true American, isn't there?"

There was a general murmur of assent. My heart thudded more loudly than ever. I did not like the sound of this. I did not like the sound of this at all.

"Hank," Henderson said, turning to Rob. "You see before you a boy. Seemingly innocent enough looking, I know. But innocence, as we all know, can be deceiving. The devil sometimes tries to fool us into believing in the innocence of an individual, when in fact that individual is laden with sin. In this case, this boy is soaked in sin. Because he is, in fact, a Jew."

I dug my fingers so hard into Chigger's coat, a smaller dog would have cried out. Chigger, however, only wagged his tail, still hoping for another crack at the bowl I held. Apparently, nobody had ever bothered to feed Chigger before. How else could you explain how easily I'd won over his allegiance?

"Hank," Henderson said. "Because you've already, in the short time I've known you, so thoroughly impressed me with your sincerity and commitment to the cause, I am going to allow you a great privilege I've heretofore denied both myself and my other men. Hank, I am going to let you kill a Jew."

And with that, Jim Henderson presented Rob with a knife he pulled out of his own boot.

A lot of things when through my mind then. I thought about how much I loved my mom, even though she can be such a pain in the ass sometimes, with her weird ideas about how I should dress and who I should date. I thought about how mad I was going to be if I didn't get to stick around to find out if Douglas ever did anything about his crush on Tasha Thompkins. I thought about the state orchestra championship, and how for the first time in years, I wouldn't be bringing home a blue ribbon cut in the shape of the state of Indiana.

It's strange the things you think about right before you die. I don't even know how I knew I was going to die. I just knew it, the way I knew that eventually, all that snow outside was going to melt, and it would be spring again someday. Rob and I were going to die, and the only thing we had to make sure of was that they didn't try to kill Seth along with us.

"Well," Henderson was saying to my boyfriend. "Go on. Take my knife. Really. It's okay. He's just a Jew."

Seth Blumenthal, I have to say, was being pretty brave. He was crying, but he was doing it quietly, with his head held high. I guess after what he'd been through, death didn't seem like such a bad thing. I don't know how else to explain it. I kind of felt the same way. I wasn't scared, really. Oh, I didn't want it to hurt. But I wasn't scared to die.

All I wanted was to take as many True Americans down with me as I could.

Rob reached out and took the knife from Jim Henderson.

"Thataboy," Henderson said, smiling in a sickly way beneath his mustache. "Now go ahead. Show us you are true believer. Stick it to the pig."

So Rob did the only thing he could. The same thing I'd have done, in his situation.

He threw an arm around Jim Henderson's neck, brought the knife blade to his jugular vein, and said, "Anybody moves, and Jimbo here gets it."

CHAPTER

14

Have you ever been to a football game where the higher ranked team was so certain of winning, there wasn't even a doubt in the minds of their fans that they wouldn't? And then, through some total miscalculation on the part of the superior team, the underdog got the upper hand?

The faces of the True Americans looked like the faces of the fans of the winning team, seconds after their team mangled some play so horribly, their opponent, against all odds, scored a touchdown.

They were stunned. Just stunned.

"Thanks," I said to Red Plaid Jacket, as I relieved him of his rifle. "I'll take that."

I had never held a rifle before in my life, but I had a pretty good idea how one worked. You just pointed at the thing you wanted to hit, and pulled the trigger. No big mystery in that.

Of course, if you thought about it, there was no reason in the world for us to be so cocky. Okay, so yeah, Rob had a knife to a guy's throat, and I had a rifle. Big deal. It was still about fifty to two. Well, three, if you counted Seth. Four, if you included Chigger, who was still following me around, hoping for more mashed potatoes, even though I'd put down the bowl.

But hey, we had the upper hand for the moment, and we were going to take advantage of it while we could.

"Okay," Rob said, as the blood slowly drained from Jim Henderson's face. Not because Rob had poked a hole in him or anything. Just because the leader of the True Americans was so very, very scared.

"Okay, now. Everybody just stay very calm, and no one is going to get hurt." Hey, he had me convinced. Rob seemed totally believable, as far as knife-wielding hostage-takers went. "Me and the girl and the kid and Jimbo here are going to take a little walk. And if any of you want to see your fearless leader live through this, you're going to let us go. Okay?"

When no one objected, Rob went, "Good. Jess. Seth. Let's go."

And so started what had to have looked like one weird parade. With me leading the way, rifle in hand and dog at my heels, a dazed-looking Seth following me, and Rob, with his arm around Henderson, taking up the rear, we made our way down the length of the barn. I wouldn't want to give you the impression that Mr. Henderson was playing the silent martyr in all of this, however. Oh, no. See, people who haven't the slightest qualm about doing unspeakably horrible things to others are always the ones who act like the biggest babies of all whenever anybody in turn threatens them.

I'm not kidding. Jim Henderson was practically crying. He was wailing, in a high-pitched voice, "You may think you're gonna get away with this, but I'll tell you what. The people are gonna rise up. The people are gonna rise up and walk the path of righteousness. And traitors like you, boy—traitors to your own race—are going to burn in hellfire for all eternity—"

"Would you," Rob said, "shut up?"

Only Jim Henderson was wrong. The people weren't going to rise up. Not all at once, anyway. They were too shocked by what was happening to their leader even to think about lifting a finger to help him. Or maybe it was just that they really did believe that if they tried anything to stop us, Rob would slit their beloved Jim Henderson's throat.

In any case, the people did not rise up.

Just one person did.

Kerchief-Head, to be exact.

I should have seen it coming. I mean, it had been way, way too easy.

But I'll admit it. I got cocky. I started thinking that these people were stupid, because they had these stupid ideas about things. That was my first mistake. Because the scariest thing about the True

Americans was that they weren't stupid. They were just really, really evil.

As became all too clear when I heard, from behind me, the sound of breaking glass.

I realized my second mistake the second I turned around. The first had been in assuming the True Americans were stupid. The second had been in not covering Rob's back with the rifle.

Because when I spun around, what I saw was Kerchief-Head standing there with two broken pieces of my mashed potato bowl in her hands. The rest of the pieces were all over the floor . . . where Rob also lay. The bitch had snuck up behind him and cracked his skull open.

Hey, I didn't hesitate. I lifted that rifle, and I fired. I didn't even think about it, I was so mad . . . mad and scared. There was a lot of blood coming out of the gash in Rob's head. More was pouring out every second.

But I had never fired a rifle before. I didn't know how they kicked. And it is not like I am this terrifically large person or anything. I pulled the trigger, the gun exploded, and the next thing I knew, I was on the floor, with Chigger licking my face and about a million and one handguns pointed at my face.

Whatever else the True Americans might have been, lacking in firearms was not one of them.

The worst part of it was, I didn't even hit Kerchief-Head. I missed her by a mile.

I did, however, manage to do some major damage to the "Don't Tread On Me" flag.

"If you've killed my boyfriend," I snarled at Kerchief-Head, as a lot of hands started grabbing me and dragging me to my feet, "I'll make you regret the day you were ever born. Do you hear me, placenta breath?"

It was childish, I knew, to stoop to name-calling. But I'm not sure I was in my right mind. I mean, Rob was lying there, completely unconscious, with all this blood making a puddle around his head. And they wouldn't let me near him. I tried to get to him. I really did. But they wouldn't let me.

Instead, they locked me up. That's right. In that little room Seth had been locked in. They threw me right in there. Me and Seth. In the dark. In the cold. With no way of knowing whether my boyfriend was dead or alive.

I don't know how much time passed before I stopped kicking the door and screaming. All I know was that the sides of my wrists hurt from where I'd pounded them against the surprisingly sturdy wood. And Seth was staring at me like I was some kind of escapee from a lunatic asylum. Really. The kid looked scared.

He looked even more scared when I said to him, "Don't worry. I'm going to get you out of here."

Well, I guess I couldn't blame him. I probably wasn't exactly giving off an aura of mature adulthood just then.

I crossed over to where he was sitting and sank down onto the bed beside him. Suddenly, I was really tired. It had been a long day.

Seth and I sat there in the dark, listening to the

distant sounds of the women banging pots and pans around in the kitchen. I guess no matter what kind of murder and mayhem was happening over in the barn, dinner still needed serving. I mean, all those men needed to keep their strength up for making the country safe for the white man, right?

Finally, after what seemed like a million years, Seth spoke. He said, in a shy voice, "I'm sorry about your friend."

I shrugged. I didn't exactly want to think about Rob. If he was dead, that was one thing. I would deal with that when the time came, probably by throwing myself headfirst into Pike's Quarry, or whatever.

But if he was still alive, and they were doing stuff to him, the way they had to Seth....

Well, let's just say that whether Rob was dead or alive, I was going to make it my sole mission in life to track down each and every one of the True Americans, and make them pay.

Preferably with a flame-thrower.

"How . . ." Seth scratched his head. He was a funny-looking kid, tall for his age, with dark hair and eyes, like me. "How did you find me, anyway?"

I looked down at my Timberlands, though I wasn't exactly seeing them, or much else, for that matter. All I could see was Rob, lying there with his head bashed in.

"I have this thing," I said, tiredly.

"A thing?" Seth asked.

"A psychic thing," I said. Which is another thing. If Rob were dead, wouldn't I know it? I mean, wouldn't I feel it? I was pretty sure I would.

But I didn't. I didn't feel anything. Except really, really tired.

"Really?" In the moonlight, Seth's face looked way younger than his thirteen years. "Hey, that's right. You're that girl. That lightning girl. I thought I'd seen you before somewhere. You were on the news."

"That's me," I said. "Lightning Girl."

"That is so cool," Seth said, admiringly.

"It's not so cool," I told him.

"No," Seth said. "It is. It really is. It's like you've got kid LoJack, or something."

"Yeah," I said. "And look what good it's done for me. You and I are stuck in here, and my boyfriend's out there bleeding to death, and another kid is dead, and possibly a cop, too—"

I saw his face crumble, and only then realized what I had said. I had let my personal grief get the better of me, and spoken out of turn. I bit my lip.

"You said he was all right," Seth said, his dark eyes suddenly swimming in tears. "That cop. You said he was okay."

"He is okay," I said, putting my arm around the little guy. "He is, really. Sorry. I just lost it for a minute there."

"He's not okay," Seth wailed. "He's dead, isn't he? And because of me! All because of me!"

It was kind of amazing that after what this kid had been through, the only thing that really got him upset was the idea that a cop that had been trying to save him had ended up catching a bullet for his troubles. Seth Blumenthal, bar mitzvah boy, really was something else.

"No, not because of you," I assured him. "Because of those asshole True Americans. And besides, he isn't dead, all right? I mean, he's hurt bad, but he isn't dead. I swear."

But Seth clearly didn't believe me. And why should he? I hadn't exactly been the most truthworthy person he'd ever met, had I? I'd told him I was there to rescue him, only instead of rescuing him, now I was just as much a prisoner as he was. I'll tell you what, I was starting to agree with him: As a rescuer, I pretty much sucked.

I was just thinking these pleasant thoughts as the door to the room we were locked in suddenly opened. I blinked as the light from the hallway, which seemed unnaturally bright thanks to my eyes having adjusted to the dimness of our cell, flooded the room. Then a figure in the doorway blocked out the light.

"Well, now." I recognized Jim Henderson's Southern twang. "Ain't that cozy, now, the two of you. Like something out of a picture postcard."

I took my arm away from Seth's shoulders and stood up. With my vision having grown accustomed to the light from the hallway, I was able to see that Henderson looked slightly disconcerted as I did this, on account of him being only an inch or two taller than me.

"Where's Rob?" I demanded.

Henderson looked confused. "Rob? Who's Rob?" Then comprehension dawned. "Oh, you mean *Hank*? Your friend with the smart mouth? Oh, I'm sorry. He's dead."

My nose was practically level with his. It took everything I had in me not to head-butt the jerk.

"I don't believe you," I said.

"Well, you better start believing me, honey," Henderson said. His eyes, blue as they were, seemed to have trouble focusing, I noticed. He had what I, having been in enough fights with people who have them, call crazy eyes. His gaze was all over the place, sometimes on the boarded-up windows behind me, sometimes on Seth, sometimes on the ceiling, but rarely, rarely where it should have been: on mine.

See? Crazy eyes.

Unfortunately, I knew from experience that there was no predicting what someone with crazy eyes was going to do next. Generally, it was just about the last thing you'd expect.

I'd have taken my chances and reached out and wrapped Jim Henderson's crazy-eyed neck into a headlock if it hadn't been for Red Plaid Jacket standing there in the hallway behind him. Red Plaid had retrieved his rifle, and had it pointed casually at me. This was discouraging, to say the least. I had a bad feeling his aim was probably better than mine.

"You know," Henderson said. "It's not just minorities like the Jews and the blacks who are ruining this country. It's people like you and your boyfriend back there. Traitors to your own race. People like you who are ashamed of the whiteness of your skin, instead of being proud—proud!—to be members of God's chosen race."

"The only time I'm ashamed to be a member of the white race," I said, "is when I'm around freaking lunatics like you."

"See," Henderson said to Kerchief-Head, who was behind Red Plaid, and was watching her leader's dealings with me with great interest. "See what happens when the liberal media gets their hands on our children? That's why I don't allow the sons and daughters of the True Americans to watch TV. No movies or radio, neither, or any of that noise people like you call music. No newspapers, no magazines. Nothing to fog the mind and cloud the judgment."

I couldn't believe he was standing there giving me a lecture. What was this, school? Hello, get on with the torture already. I swear I'd have rather been held down and branded than listen to this dude's random crap much longer.

But unfortunately, he wasn't through.

"Who sent you?" Henderson asked me. "Tell me who you work for. The CIA? FBI? Who?"

I burst out laughing, though of course there wasn't anything too funny about the situation.

"I don't work for anybody," I said. "I came here for Seth."

Henderson shook his head. "So young," he said. "Yet so full of lies. America doesn't belong to people like you, you know," he went on.

"America is for pioneers like us, people willing to work the land, people who aren't afraid to get their hands dirty."

"You certainly proved that," I remarked, "when you killed Nate Thompkins. Can't get much dirtier than that."

Henderson smiled. But again, thanks to the crazy eyes, the smile didn't quite reach all the way to those baby blues of his.

"The black boy, you mean? Yes, well, it was necessary to leave a warning, in case any more people of his persuasion took it into their heads to move to this area. You see, it's important for us to keep the land pure for our children, the sons and daughters of the True Americans."

"Well, congratulations," I said. "I bet your kids are gonna be real happy about what you did to Nate, especially when they're frying your butt for murder up in Indianapolis. I know how proud I'd be to have a convicted felon for a dad."

"I don't worry about laws made by man," Mr. Crazy Eyes informed me with a smile. "I worry only about divine law, laws handed down by God."

"Huh," I said. "Then you're gonna be in for a surprise. Because I'm pretty sure 'Thou Shalt Not Kill' came straight from the big guy himself."

But Jim just shook his head. "It's only a sin to kill those God created in his own image. In other words, white men," he explained, tiredly. "People like you will never understand." He sighed. "Living as you always have in the comforts of the city, never knowing what it is to work the soil—"

"I've got news for you," I said. "There are a lot of people I know who don't live in town and who've worked the soil plenty but who feel the same way about you freaks that I do."

He went on like he hadn't heard me. Who knew? Maybe he hadn't. Clearly Mr. Henderson was only hearing what he wanted to hear anyway.

"Americans have always dealt with adversity. From the savages they encountered upon their arrival to this great land, and then from foreign influences who threatened to destroy them. Pretty ironic, ain't it, that the greatest threat of all comes not from forces overseas, but from within the country of America itself."

"Whatever," I said. I'd had about as much as I could take. "Are you here to mess me up, or what?"

Crazy Eyes finally looked me full in the face.

"You will be disposed of," he said, in a voice as cold as the wind outside. "You, your boyfriend, and the Jew will all be disposed of, the same way we disposed of the black boy. Your bodies will be left as a warning to any who doubt that the new age has arrived, and that the battle has begun. You see, someone has got to fight for this great nation. Someone has got to keep America safe for our children, prevent it from succumbing to hate and greed. . . ."

The great Jim Henderson broke off as, from

outside the ranch house, an enormous explosion—rather like the kind that might occur if someone threw a lit cigarette down a trailer's septic tank—rocked the compound.

I smiled sweetly up into Jim Henderson's crazy eyes and said, "Uh, Mr. Henderson? Yeah, I think that someone you were talking about, the one who is going to make America safe for our children? Yeah. He and his friends just arrived. And from the sound of it, you've really pissed them off."

CHAPTER

15

And then I hauled off and slugged him. Right between those crazy, shifty eyes.

It hurt like hell, because mostly what my knuckles caught was bone. But I didn't care. I'd been wanting to punch that guy for a long, long time. The pain was totally worth it, especially when, as I'd known he would, Henderson crumpled up like a doll, and fell, wailing, to the floor.

"She hit me," he cried. "She hit me! Don't just stand there, Nolan! Do something. The bitch hit me!"

Nolan—aka Red Plaid Jacket—was too busy squawking into his Walkie-Talkie however to pay attention to his fearless leader. "We got incoming! Do you copy, Blue Leader? We are under attack. Do you copy? Do you copy?"

Red Plaid might have been more interested in what was happening to the rest of the compound, but that certainly wasn't the case with Kerchief-Head. She was pretty hacked that I'd taken a poke at her spiritual guide—hey, for all I know, Henderson might even have been her honey. She could easily have been Mrs. Henderson.

I was hopping around, waving my sore knuckles, when Kerchief-Head, with a snarl that would have put Chigger to shame, launched herself at me.

"Ain't nobody gonna do Jim like that," she declared, as her not-insignificant weight struck me full force, and sent me back against the bed, pinned beneath her.

Mrs. Henderson—if that's who she really was—was a big woman, all right, but she had the disadvantage of not having been in many fights before. That was clear from the fact that she did not go directly for my eyes, as someone better accustomed to confronting adversaries would have.

Plus, for all her doughiness, Mrs. Henderson wasn't very muscular. I easily twisted to sink a knee into her stomach, then accompanied that by a quick thrust of one elbow into the back of her neck while she was sunk over, clutching her gut. And that took care of Kerchief-Head.

Meanwhile, outside, another explosion ripped through the compound.

"Save the children," Kerchief-Head gasped. "Somebody save the children!"

Like Chick and those guys would even be targeting the kids. I am so sure.

"Who do you people think we are?" I demanded. "*You?*"

Then I reached out, grabbed Seth by the arm, and said, "Come on."

We would have gotten safely out of there, too, if I'd just hit Henderson a little harder. Unfortunately, however, he recovered all too quickly from my punch . . . or at least quickly enough to reached out and wrap a hand around my ankle, just as we were stepping over him.

"You ain't goin' nowhere," Jim Henderson breathed. I was delighted to note that blood was streaming from his nose. Not as much blood as had streamed from Rob's head, but a fairly satisfying amount, nonetheless.

"It's all over, Mr. Henderson," I said. "You better let go now, or you're going to regret it."

"You stupid bitch," Henderson wheezed. He couldn't talk too well, on account of the blood and mucous flowing into his mouth thanks to what I'd done to his nose. "You have no idea what you've done. You think you've done this country a favor, but all you've done is sign its death warrant."

"Hey, Mr. Henderson—" Seth said.

When the crazy-eyed man looked up at him, the boy brought his foot down with all the force he had on the hand that was grasping my ankle.

"—eat my shorts."

Henderson, with another cry of pain, released me at once. And Seth and I took off down the hallway.

Red Plaid Jacket, aka Nolan, had disappeared. There were plenty of other people, however, creating chaos in the ranch house. Women and children were darting around like goldfish in a bowl, calling each other's names and falling over one another. I couldn't blame them for panicking, really. The acrid smell of smoke was already thick in the air, and it got even thicker when Seth and I finally burst outside . . .

. . . to be greeted with the welcome sight of Jim Henderson's barn and meeting house in flames.

Both trailers were on fire, as well. All around the snowy yard ran True Americans, waving rifles and looking panicked. The panic wasn't just because most of their compound was on fire. It was also because extremely large men, many of whom were wearing cowboy hats, were whipping back and forth across the yard on the backs of snowmobiles. It was a truly magnificent sight, seeing those sleek vehicles sailing over the snow in direct pursuit of an overalled True American. I saw Red Plaid Jacket try to take aim at one with his rifle. Too bad for him that the minute he did, another snowmobiler, yelling, "Yeehaw!" darted forward and knocked the gun right out of his hands.

Meanwhile, not far away, another snowmobiler had lassoed an escaping True American neatly as if he'd been a fleeing heifer, bringing him down to the snow with a satisfying thud. Elsewhere, two snowmobilers had cornered a pair of Jim Henderson's followers, and were just gliding around and around them, giving them a tiny bit of room to escape, then cutting off that escape route at just the last moment, entirely for kicks.

"Whoa," Seth said, his eyes very wide. "Who *are* these guys?"

I sighed happily, my heart filled with joy.

"Grits," I said.

And then I remembered Rob. Rob, who, last I'd seen him, had been spread-eagle on the floor of the True Americans' meeting house.

Which was now in flames.

I forgot about Seth. I forgot about Jim Henderson and Chick and the True Americans. All I thought about was getting to Rob, and as fast as humanly possible.

Unfortunately, that meant running across the snow toward a burning building while Hell's Angels and truckers on snowmobiles were ripping the place apart. It was a wonder I got as far I did. Part of it was due to the fact that Chigger appeared from out of nowhere, and, apparently thinking I still had mashed potatoes on me that he might be able to score, loped after me.

I didn't recognize him right away, however— there were other dogs running around the place, barking their heads off thanks to all the shooting—and I thought he'd been trying to bring me down. So I kicked up my heels, let me tell you.

But when I got to the barn doors and peered inside, all I could see were flames. The tables were on fire. The rafters were on fire. Even the walls were on fire. Though I couldn't lean in very far, due to the extreme heat, I could see that no one was inside . . . not even any unconscious motorbike mechanics who happened to be on probation.

Then I was suddenly yanked off my feet. Thinking a True American had gotten hold of me, I lashed out with my feet and fists. But then a familiar voice went, "Simmer down, there, little lady! It's me, old Chick! What choo want to do, light your hair on fire? Get away from those flames, they're hot!"

"Chick!" I squirmed around in his arms until I was facing him. He was barely recognizable in his winter gear, which included a thick pair of aviation goggles. But I didn't care how he looked. I had never been so happy to see anyone in my life.

"Chick, have you seen Rob? They got him. The True Americans, I mean. They got Rob!"

Chick looked bored. "Wilkins is fine," he said, jerking a thumb at a rusted-out pickup sitting half-buried in snow about twenty yards away. "I put 'im in the back of that old Chevy. He's still out like a light, but it don't look too bad."

I clung to the front of his leather jacket, hardly daring to believe my ears. "But the blood," I said. "There was so much of it. . . ."

"Aw," Chick said, disgustedly. "Wilkins was always one to bleed like a stuck pig. Don't worry about him. He's got a head like a rock. He'll be all right, after a coupla stitches. Now what about this kid? Where's he?"

I looked around, and saw Seth still standing over by the ranch house door, shivering in the winter cold despite the heat from the many fires all around him.

"Over there," I said, pointing.

At that moment, a shot rang out. I ducked instinctively, but ended up with my face in the snow, thanks to Chick practically throwing me to the ground, then trying to shield me with his own body.

"Idiots," he muttered, not seeming the least discomfited by the fact that he was laying on top of a girl he hardly knew. "Told those boys we had to take out their muni shed first. But they said no way would the fools shoot at us with women and children around. They're true Americans, all right. True American assholes. Damn! You all right?"

I could barely breathe, he was so heavy. "Fine," I grunted. "Seth. Got to get Seth . . . out of range . . . of gunfire."

"I'm on it," Chick said. Then, mercifully, he climbed off me, and back onto his snowmobile. "You get on over to Wilkins," he said. "I'll get the kid and meet up with you, then we'll figure out a way to get the three of you outta this hellhole."

He took off with a spray of snow and gravel. I was still spitting tiny ice particles out from between my teeth when I heard a strange noise and looked down.

Chigger was still with me, and was doing the exact same thing I was—trying to get rid of all the snow and bits of dirt clinging to his hair.

I had, I realized, a new friend.

"Come on, boy," I said to him, and the two of us raced for the abandoned pickup.

They'd wrapped Rob in something yellow, then laid him out across the bed of the pickup. I scrambled up into it, Chigger following close behind. It wasn't so easy to see Rob's face in the dark, but there was still enough glow from the moon—not to mention the many fires all around us—for me to make out the fact that, as Chick had promised, he was still breathing, deeply and regularly. The wound on his head had stopped bleeding, and didn't look anywhere as serious as it had back in the barn. There it had looked like a hole. Now I could see that it was merely a gash, barely an inch wide.

Which was lucky for Mrs. Henderson. Because if she'd given my boyfriend brain damage, that would have been the end of her.

"It's okay," I said to Rob, brushing some of his dark hair from his forehead, and carefully kissing the place on his face that was the least smeared with blood. "I'm here now. Everything's going to be all right."

At least that's what I believed then. That was right before I heard the deep rumble in Chigger's throat, and looked up to see a wild man standing beside the pickup, his arms raised, and his face hidden by all his long, straggly hair.

Okay, okay. That's just what it looked like at first. I realize there's no such thing as wild men, or Sasquatch, or Bigfoot or whatever. But seriously, for a minute, that's what I thought this guy was. I mean, he was completely covered in snow, and standing there with his arms out like that, what was I supposed to think? I screamed my head off.

I think Chigger would have gone for the guy's throat if he hadn't waved the hands he had extended toward me and cried, "Jessica! It's me! Dr. Krantz." I grabbed hold of Chigger's thick leather collar at the last possible minute and kept him from leaping from the cab bed to Cyrus Krantz's neck.

"Jeez!" I said, sinking back onto my heels in relief. "Dr. Krantz, what is wrong with you? Don't you know better than to sneak up on people like that?"

Dr. Krantz flipped back his enormous, fur-trimmed hood and blinked at me through the fogged-up lenses of his glasses.

"Jessica, are you all right?" he wanted to know. "I was so worried! When these animals on the snowmobiles showed up, I thought I'd lost you for sure—"

"Take it easy, Doc," I said. "The guys on the snowmobiles are on our side. What are you doing here, anyway? I thought I told you to go home."

"Jessica," Dr. Krantz said, severely. "You can't honestly think I would leave you out here in the middle of nowhere, can you? Your welfare is extremely important to me, Jessica. To the whole Bureau, in fact."

"Uh, yeah, Dr. Krantz," I said. "And that's why you're out here on your own. Because the Bureau was so concerned for my welfare, they sent out backup right away."

Dr. Krantz pulled a cell phone from his pocket. "I tried to call for help," he explained, sheepishly, "but there must not be any relay centers this far into the woods. I can't get a signal."

"Huh," I said. "That'll make Jim Henderson happy. He's all against contact with the outside world, you know. It infects the youth with liberal ideas."

"This Henderson is an extremely unsavory character, Jessica," Dr. Krantz said. "I can't understand why you felt compelled to take him and his lot on all by yourself. You could have come to us, you know. We would gladly have helped."

"Well," I said. I didn't mention that I hadn't been too impressed by the way Dr. Krantz and his fellow law enforcement officers had handled the True Americans so far. "What's done is done. Look, Doc, I gotta get Rob to a hospital. Do you think you could help me carry him to your car? I know he's heavy, but I'm stronger than I look, and maybe between the two of us—"

But Dr. Krantz was already shaking his head.

"Oh," he said. "But I didn't drive out here, Jessica. It would be quite impossible to get an automobile way out here. The way is virtually impassable thanks to the snow, and besides, there aren't really any proper roadways to speak of. I suppose that is part of the allure of places like these for folks like Jim Henderson—"

"Wait a minute," I said. "If you didn't drive, how did you follow us out here?"

Dr. Krantz, for the first time since I'd met him, actually looked a little embarrassed.

"Well, you see, I followed you in my car as far as that extraordinary little bar you went to. Chick's, I believe it is called? And then when I saw the two of you—you and Mr. Wilkins—leave by snowmobile, why, I got my skis out of the trunk and followed your tracks."

I stared at him. "Your *what?*" ·

"My skis." Dr. Krantz cleared his throat. "Cross-country skiing is one of the finest forms of cardio-vascular exercise, so I always keep my skis with me in the winter months, because you never know when an opportunity might arise to—"

"You're telling me," I interrupted, "that you skied all the way here. You. Cyrus Krantz. Skied here."

"Well," Dr. Krantz said. "Yes. It wasn't far, really. Only twenty miles or so, which is nothing to a well-conditioned skier, which I happen to be. And really, I don't think it at all as extraordinary as you're making it out to be. Skiing is a perfectly viable form of exercise—"

When the shots rang out, that's what we were doing. Talking about skiing. Cross-country ski-ing, to be exact, and its viability as a form of car-diovascular exercise. One minute I was sitting there next to Rob, listening to Dr. Krantz, a guy that, it had to be admitted, up until then I really hadn't liked too well.

And the next, I was talking to air, because one of the bullets the True Americans sent flying in my direction pierced Dr. Krantz, and sent him flying.

CHAPTER

16

It was my fault, really. My fault because I'd known people were shooting off guns, and I hadn't mentioned anything to Dr. Krantz like, "Oh, by the way, look out for flying bullets," or, "Hadn't you better stand behind this truck instead of in front of it? It might make better cover."

Nope. I didn't say a word.

And the next thing I knew, the guy was curled up in the snow beside the pickup, screaming his head off.

Well, if you'd been shot, you'd have screamed your head off, too.

I was out of the cab bed and into the snow beside him in a split second.

"Let me see," I said. I could tell the bullet had gotten him in the leg, because he was clutching it with both hands and rocking back and forth, screaming.

Dr. Krantz didn't let me see, though. He just kept rocking and screaming. Meanwhile all these spurts of blood were coming out from between his gloved fingers, and hitting the snow all around us, making these designs that were actually kind of pretty.

But you know, I took first aid in the sixth grade, and when blood is spurting out that hard and that far, it means something is really wrong. Like maybe the bullet had hit an artery or whatever.

So I did the only thing I could do, under the circumstances.

I punched Dr. Krantz in the jaw.

I felt pretty bad about it, but what else could I do? The guy was hysterical. He wouldn't let me look at the wound. He could have bled to death.

After I hit him, though, he kind of fell back in the snow, and I got a good look at the damage the bullet had done. Too good a look, if you ask me. Just as I suspected, the bullet had severed an artery—I can't remember what it's called, but it's that one in the thigh. A pretty big one, too.

Fortunately for Dr. Krantz, however, I was on the case.

"Listen," I said, to him, as he lay in the snow, moaning. "You are in luck. I did my sixth grade science fair project on tourniquets."

For some reason, this did not seem to reassure Dr. Krantz as it should have. He started moaning harder.

"No, really," I told him. I had pulled his coat

up, and was undoing the belt to his pants. I was relieved to see he was wearing one. I know I sure wasn't. Though I could have used one of the laces from my Timberlands in a pinch.

"My best thing," I told him, "was tourniquets made from found objects. You know, like if you were out camping, and a big stick went through you, or whatever. You know. Maybe you wouldn't have a first aid kit with you." I ducked, and looked under the pickup. As I'd hoped, the snow wasn't so deep beneath it. I was able to find a good-sized rock . . . not too big, but not too small, either. Artery sized. I tried to get the dirt off it as best I could.

"The major thing you have to worry about," I assured Dr. Krantz—it's important that you talk to a victim of a major injury like this one, in order to keep him from slipping into shock—"isn't secondary infection so much as blood loss. So I know this rock looks dirty, but—" I jammed the rock into the wound in Dr. Krantz's leg. The blood stopped spurting almost right away. "—it's performing a vital function. You know. Keeping your blood in."

I took Dr. Krantz's belt, and looped the other end through the belt buckle, then pulled until the belt buckle wedged the rock deeper into the wound. I wasn't too thrilled about having to do this, but it didn't help that Dr. Krantz screamed so loud. I mean, I felt bad enough. Besides, all the screaming was making Chigger, still in the cab bed with Rob, whine nervously.

"There," I said to Dr. Krantz. "That will keep the rock in place. Now we just need to find a stick, so we can twist the belt, and cut off the circulation—"

"No," Dr. Krantz said, in what sounded more like his normal voice—although it was still ragged with pain. "No stick. For the love of God, no stick."

I looked critically down at my handiwork.

"I don't know," I said. "I mean, we may not be able to save the leg, Dr. Krantz. But at least you won't bleed to death."

"No stick," Dr. Krantz gasped. "I'm begging you."

I didn't like it, but I didn't see what else I could do. Fortunately at that moment, Chick sped up to us, Seth clinging tightly to his waist.

"What the hell happened?" Chick was down off his snowmobile and into the snow beside us in a flash. For a big man, he could move like the wind when he needed to. "Christ, I leave you alone for a second, and—"

"Somebody shot him," I said, looking down at Dr. Krantz's leg, which, truth be told, looked a lot like a raw hamburger. "He won't let me use a stick."

"No stick," Dr. Krantz hissed, through gritted teeth.

Chick was examining my field tourniquet with interest. "For torsion, you mean?" When I nodded, he said, "I don't think you need it. Looks like you've got the bleeding stopped for now.

Listen, though, we don't have much time. You gotta get this guy out of here. Wilkins, too. And the little guy." He nodded his head at Seth, who was looking owlishly down at the crazy pattern of blood in the snow, as if it were the worst thing he had ever seen. As if what had happened to his own hand was just, you know, incidental.

"I know," I said. "But how am I going to do that? Dr. Krantz can't drive a snowmobile. Not in his condition. And Rob'd never stay on one. . . ."

"That's why—" Chick stood up, and started for the front of the pickup. "—you gotta take the truck."

I looked skeptically at the ancient vehicle. "I don't even know if it runs," I said. "And even if it does, I don't know where we'd find the keys."

"Don't need keys," Chick said, opening the driver's door, then ducking beneath the dash, "when Chick is on the case."

I looked over my shoulder. Up the hill from us, the flames from the barn now seemed to be reaching almost to the moon. Thick black smoke trailed into the sky, blocking out the cold twinkle of the Milky Way. True Americans were still running around, shooting off guns. I could dimly make out the small figure of Jim Henderson waving his arms at his brethren. He seemed to be encouraging them to fight harder.

Behind me, the pickup suddenly sputtered to life.

"There ya go," Chick said, with a chuckle. He came out from beneath the dash and blew on his fingertips before slipping his gloves back on. "Oh, yeah," he said. "I still got the touch."

I stared at him, as wide-eyed as poor Seth.

"Wait a minute," I said. "You want me to *drive* these guys out of here?"

"That's the general idea," Chick said, not looking very perturbed.

"But there's no road!" I burst out. "You told me over and over, there's no road to this place."

"Well," Chick said, reaching up to stroke his beard. "No, you got that right. There ain't no road, exactly."

"So just how—" I realized Seth, along with Dr. Krantz, was listening to us with a great deal of interest. I reached out, grabbed Chick by the arm, and started walking him away from the truck, lowering my voice as I continued. "—am I supposed to get them back to town, if there's no road?"

It was at that exact moment that something in the barn blew up. I don't know what it was exactly, but I had a feeling it was that muni supply Chick had been talking about. Suddenly, tiny bits of metal and wood were raining down on us.

Chick let out a stream of very colorful expletives that I was just barely able to hear above all the explosions. Then he darted around to the pickup and hauled a protesting Dr. Krantz to his one good foot.

"Sorry, girlie," Chick yelled at me, as he dragged Dr. Krantz around the truck and started stuffing him into the passenger seat. "But you gotta get these folks outta here before all hell breaks loose."

"*Before?*" I couldn't believe any of this was happening. "Um, correct me if I'm wrong, but from the looks of things, I think it already has."

"What?" Chick screamed at me, as the sky was lit a brilliant orange and red.

"Hell," I yelled back. "I think we're already in it!"

"Aw, this is nothing." Chick slammed the door on Dr. Krantz, then hurried around to make sure Rob was secure in the cab bed. "Kid," he yelled at Seth. "Get in here and make sure this guy don't slide around too much. And shield him from that crap flying around, would ya?"

Seth, white-faced but resolute, did as Chick asked without a single question. He climbed into the back of the pickup and knelt down beside Rob . . . after giving Chigger a few wary looks, that is.

Then, taking me by the elbow, Chick pointed down the hill, into the thick black copse of trees that separated Jim Henderson's property from the county road far, far below.

"You just head straight down," he yelled, as, up by the ranch house, what I could have sworn was machine-gun fire broke out. "So long as you're going down, you're headed for the road. Understand?"

I nodded miserably. "But, Chick," I couldn't help adding. "The snow—"

"Right," Chick said, with a nod. "It's gonna be more of a slalom than a drive. Just remember, if you get into trouble, pump the brakes. And try not to hit anything head on."

"Oh," I said, bitterly. "Thanks for the advice. This may not be the right time to bring this up, but you know, I don't even have a driver's license."

"That guy's leg ain't gonna wait," Chick told me. "And Wilkins won't last long out here, neither." Then, perhaps noting my nauseous expression, he slapped me on the shoulder and said, "You'll be fine. Now get going."

Then he hoisted me in the air and set me down behind the wheel, beside a panting, sweating Dr. Krantz.

"Uh," I said, to Dr. Krantz. "How you doin', Doc?"

Dr. Krantz gave a queasy look.

"Oh," he said. "I'm just great."

Chick tapped on the closed window between us. With some effort, I managed to get it rolled down.

"One more thing." Chick reached under his leather jacket and drew out a stubby black object. It took me a minute to realize what it was. When I did, I nearly threw up.

"Oh, no!" I said, putting out both hands, as if to ward him off. "You get that thing away from me."

Chick merely stuck his arm through the open window and deposited the object on my lap.

"Anyone comes near you or the truck," he said, not loudly enough for Dr. K to hear, but loudly enough for me to hear him over the sound of gunfire behind us, "you shoot. Understand?"

"Chick," I said, looking down at the gun, and feeling sicker than ever. It had been one thing when I'd try to blow Kerchief-Head away. That had been in the heat of the moment. But this . . .

"Hey," Chick said. "You think Henderson's the only crazy in these woods? Not by a long shot. And he's got a lot of friends. You just drive, you'll be all right. Only shoot if you have to."

I nodded. I didn't dare look at Dr. Krantz.

"Remember," Chick said through the driver's side window. "Pump the brakes."

"Sure," I said, still feeling like throwing up.

Chick smacked the rusted hood, knocking off several inches of snow, and said, "Get going, then."

Fighting back my nausea, I rolled up the window then glanced through the rear windshield and yelled to Seth, "You ready back there?"

Seth, his arms around Rob's shoulders, nodded. Beside him, Chigger sat with his tongue lolling, happy to be going for a ride.

"Ready," Seth yelled.

I looked beside me. Dr. Krantz did not look good. For one thing, he was in a pretty awkward position, with one leg stretched out at an odd angle in front of him. The lenses of his glasses were completely fogged up, he was almost as pale as the snow outside his window. But he was still conscious, and I guess that's all that mattered.

"Ready, Dr. Krantz?" I asked.

He nodded tensely.

"Just do it," he rasped.

So I put my foot on the gas. . . .

CHAPTER

17

Once when we were little, Ruth had a birthday party at the Zoom Floom. The Zoom Floom was located on the same hillside as Paoli Peaks Ski Resort. It was a water slide that only operated in summertime. The way you went down it was, you laid down on this rubber mat, and an attendant pushed you off.

Then, suddenly, you were plummeting down a mountain, with about fifty billion tons of water pushing you even faster downward, and when you opened your mouth to scream, all of that water got into your mouth, and you went around these hairpin curves that seemed like they might kill you, and usually your mat slipped out from under you and you were skidding down the slide with just your suit on. And the surface of the slide was rough enough to take the skin off your hipbones, and with every second you were certain you were to going drown or at least crack your head open, until at last you plunged into this four-foot-deep pool at the bottom and came up choking and gasping for air, only to be hit in the head by your mat a moment or two later.

And then you grabbed your mat and started up the stairs to go again. You had to. Because it was so freaking fun.

But sliding down the wooded hill from Jim Henderson's militia compound? Yeah, so not fun.

And if we lived through it—which I doubted we would? Yeah, so never doing it again.

I realized pretty early on as we plunged straight at the pine trees that formed a thick wall around the True Americans' compound that Chick was right about one thing: The plows certainly hadn't been near Jim Henderson's place. I found the road pretty quickly—or what passed for a road, apparently, in the opinion of the True Americans. It was really just a track between the pine trees, the branches of many of which hung so low, they brushed against the top of the cab as we went by.

But the snow that lay across the so-called road was thick, and beneath it seemed to be a real nice layer of ice. As the truck careened down the hillside path, branches whipping against it, causing Seth and Chigger, in the back, to duck down low, it took every ounce of strength I had just to control the wheel, to keep the front tires from spinning out and sending us—oh, yes—into the deep ravine to my left. A ravine that I was quite sure in summertime made a charming fishing and swimming hole, but which now appeared to me, as I barreled alongside it, without even a token guardrail between it and me, a pit to hell.

All this, of course, was only visible to me thanks to the moonlight, which was fortunately generous. I had the truck's brights on, but in a way that only made things worse, because then I could plainly see every near-catastrophe looming before us. I probably would have been better off just closing my eyes, for all the good my jerking on the wheel and pumping the brakes, as Chick had suggested, seemed to be doing me.

None of this was helped by the fact that all the jolting seemed to have brought Dr. Krantz out from his state of semi-consciousness. He was awake, all right, and hanging on for dear life to the dashboard. There were no seatbelts in the cab—apparently, passenger safety was not of primary concern to the True Americans. Dr. Krantz was being jounced all over the place, and there wasn't a blessed thing I could do about it . . . or about Rob and Seth, in the back, who were receiving the same nice treatment.

I have to admit though that Dr. Krantz wasn't helping very much by grabbing his leg with the tourniquet on it and sucking air in between his teeth every time we passed over a particularly large rock in the road, hidden beneath all that snow. I mean, I know it must have hurt and all, but hello, I was driving. I kept glancing over to make sure the tourniquet was still tight. I had to, since he hadn't let me torque it off.

I was glancing over at Dr. Krantz's leg when I suddenly heard him suck in his breath, and not because we'd gone over a bump. I quickly glanced through the windshield, but could see nothing more horrifying that what we'd already encountered, treacherous drop-offs and looming trees. Then I heard a tap at the back window, and turned my head.

Seth, white-faced and panicked-looking, pointed behind him.

"We got company!" he yelled.

I glanced in the rearview mirror—then realized that, disobeying one of the first rules of driving, I had not thought to adjust my mirrors before I put my foot on the gas. I couldn't see squat out of them, thanks to their having been tilted for a much taller person than me.

Reaching up, I grasped the rearview mirror and tried to adjust it so that I could see what was behind us, while at the same time navigating a ten-foot dip in the road that sent all of us airborne for a second or two. . . .

And then I saw it. Two True Americans barreling after us in a four by four. A pretty new one, too, if you asked me. And these guys seemed to know what they were doing. They were gaining on us already, and I hadn't even noticed their headlights, which meant they couldn't have been behind us for all that long.

I did the only thing I could, under the circumstances. I floored it.

This strategy, apparently, was not one Dr. Krantz seemed prepared to fully embrace.

"For God's sake, Jessica," he said, speaking for the first time since being put in the cab. "You're going to kill us all."

"Yeah," I said, keeping my eyes on the road. "Well, what do you think these guys are going to do to us if they catch us?"

"There's another way," Dr. Krantz said. "Give me that gun."

I nearly cracked up laughing at that one. "No freaking way."

"Jessica." Dr. Krantz sounded mad. "There's no alternative."

"You are not," I said, "starting a shootout with those guys with my boyfriend and Seth in the back there, completely unprotected. Sorry."

Dr. Krantz shook his head. "Jessica, I assure you. I am an expert marksman."

"Yeah, but I'll bet they aren't." I nodded toward the rearview mirror. "And if they start aiming for you, chances are, they're going to hit me. Or Seth. Or Rob. So you can forget"—We hit a particularly large bump in the road and went flying for a second or two—"about it."

Dr. Krantz, it was clear, wasn't about to forget about it. Fortunately, however, that last bump sent him into paroxysms of pain, so he was too busy to think about the gun for a little while. . . .

But not too busy to see, as I soon did, the horrifying sight that loomed before us. And that was a large portion of the road that had disappeared.

That's right, disappeared, as if it had never been there. It took me a minute or two to realize that what it was, in fact, was a small wooden bridge that, undoubtedly due to rotting wood, had collapsed under the weight of all that snow. Now there was a six-foot-wide gap between this side of the ravine and the far side . . . the side to medical care for Rob and Dr. Krantz. And to freedom.

"Slow down!" Dr. Krantz screamed. I swear, if his leg closest to me hadn't been all busted up, he would have tried to reach over with it and slam down the brakes himself. "Jessica, don't you see it?"

I saw it all right. But what I saw was our one chance to get away from these clowns.

Which was why I pressed down on that gas pedal for all I was worth.

"Hang on!" I screamed at Seth.

Dr. Krantz threw his arms out to brace himself against the roof of the cab and the dashboard, as the ravine loomed ever closer. "Jessica!" he yelled. "You are insane—"

And then the wheels of the pickup left the ground, and we were flying. Really. Just like in dreams. You know the ones, where you dream you can fly? And while you're in the air, it's totally quiet, and all you can hear is your heartbeat, and you don't even dare breathe because if you do, you might drop down to the ground again, and you don't want that to happen because what you are experiencing is a miracle, the miracle of flight, and you want to make it last as long as you possibly can. . . .

And then, with a crash, we were down again, on the far side of the ravine . . . and still going, faster than ever. Only the jolt of our landing had sent all of our bones grinding together—I know I bit my tongue—not to mention, it seemed to blow the shocks out of the truck. It certainly blew something out, since the truck shimmied all over, then made a pathetic whining sound. . . .

But it kept going. I kept my foot to that gas pedal, and that truck kept on going.

"Oh my God," Dr. Krantz kept saying. "Oh my God, oh my God, oh my God, oh my God. . . ."

Cyrus, I knew, was gone. I dared a glance over my shoulder, as the truck ground up a steep incline on the far side of the ravine we'd jumped.

"You guys okay back there?" I yelled, and was relieved to see Seth's white face, and Chigger's laughing one, right there.

"We lost 'em!" Seth yelled, triumphantly. "Look!"

I looked. And Seth was right. The four by four had tried the same jump we had, but hadn't been able to get up as much speed as we had. Now it lay with its crumpled nose in the creek bed, the two men inside struggling to get out.

Something burst from within me. Suddenly, I was yelling, "Yeehaw!" like a cowboy. I never lifted my foot off the gas, but it was all I could do to stay in my seat behind that wheel. I wanted to jump out and kiss everyone in sight. Even Dr. Krantz. Even Chigger.

And then, without warning, we were bursting through the trees, and sliding onto the main road. Just like that. The moon was shining down hard, reflecting off the snow carpeting the barren fields all around us. After being so deep in the dark woods, all that light was almost blinding . . . blinding and the most beautiful sight I'd ever seen. Even as I was slamming on the brakes and we went sliding across the icy highway, I was smiling happily. We'd made it! We'd really made it!

When the truck finally slid to a halt, I risked a glance at the wooded hill behind us. You couldn't tell, just by looking at it, that it housed a bunch of wacko survivalists. It just looked, you know, like a pretty wooded hill.

Except for the smoke pouring from the top of it out into the moonlit sky. Really. It kind of looked like pictures I'd seen of Mount St. Helens, right before it blew up. Only on a much smaller scale, of course.

I looked around. We were in the middle of nowhere. There wasn't a farmhouse, or even a trailer, to be seen. Certainly nowhere I could make a phone call.

Then I remembered Dr. Krantz's cell phone.

I glanced over at him, but the guy was out. I guess that last burst of speed did him in. I leaned over and pawed around in his coat for a minute, then finally located the phone inside a pocket that also contained a Palm Pilot, a pack of Juicy Fruit, and a lot of used-up Kleenex. I helped myself to a piece of the Juicy Fruit, then opened up the rear window and passed the pack, along with the cell phone, to Seth.

"Here," I said to him, as he took both. "Call your parents to let them know you're all right, and that they can pick you up in five minutes at County Medical. Then call the cops and tell them what's happening up at Jim Henderson's place. If the fire department's going to get up there, they'll need to bring a plow." Then I remembered the blown-out bridge. "And maybe a road crew," I added.

Seth, after stuffing the Juicy Fruit in his mouth, eagerly began to dial. I turned back to face the road. My arms ached from my battle with the steering wheel, and despite the cold, there was a ribbon of sweat running all up and down my chest. But we had made it. We had made it.

Almost.

I committed twenty-seven traffic violations getting Rob and Dr. Krantz to the hospital. I went thirty miles over the speed limit—forty outside of town—went through three stoplights, made an illegal left-hand turn, and went the wrong way down a one-way street. Not that it mattered much. There was practically no one out on the streets, thanks to all the snow. The only time I ran into traffic was outside the Chocolate Moose, where a lot of kids from Ernie Pyle High hang out. It was after eleven, so the Moose was closed, but there were still kids around, necking in their cars. When I blew past them, I laid on the horn, just for the fun of it. I saw a number of startled heads lift up as I flew by. I yelled, "Yeehaw," at them, and a couple of irritated jocks yelled, "Grit!" back at me. I guess because of the truck. And maybe because of the yeehaw. And quite possibly because of Chigger.

But you know what? They couldn't have called me something that filled me with more pride.

When I swung around the entrance to the hospital, I saw that I had a choice of two entrances: the one for emergency vehicles only, and the one for general admittance.

Of course I chose the one for the emergency vehicles. I figured I'd come skidding to a halt in front of it, you know, like on *The Dukes of Hazard*, and all these emergency room personnel would come running out, all concerned about hearing the brakes squeal.

Only it didn't happen quite like that, because I guess most emergency vehicles don't go skidding into that entrance very much, and even though it had been plowed and salted, there was still a lot of ice. So instead of skidding to a halt in front of the emergency room doors, I sort of ended up driving through them.

But hey. All the emergency room personnel *did* come running up, just like I'd thought they would.

Fortunately the emergency room doors were glass, so crashing into them really didn't cause that much damage to my passengers. I mean, once the front wheels hit the emergency room floor and got some traction, the brakes worked, so Seth and Rob were fine. And Dr. Krantz was unconscious anyway, so when his head hit the dashboard, it probably didn't even hurt that much. It was more like a little tap. I know that's how it felt when I was flung against the steering wheel. Fortunately the truck was so old, it didn't have air bags, so we didn't have to deal with *that* embarrassment.

Still, the people in the emergency bay were surprisingly unsympathetic to my predicament. I mean, you would think that after what I'd been through, they'd be a little more understanding, but no. They didn't act at all like the emergency room people on that show on TV.

"Are you crazy?" one nurse in blue scrubs was yelling, as I lifted my head from the steering wheel.

That made me mad. I mean, all I'd done is gotten a little glass on the floor. It wasn't like I'd run over anybody.

"Hey," I said. "There's a guy in the back of this truck with a head injury, and this guy next to me is about to lose a leg. Get a couple gurneys, then get off my back."

That shut her up, let me tell you. In seconds, it seemed, they'd gotten Dr. Krantz out of the cab, then helped me back the truck up so they could get outside, and help move Rob. Seth was able to climb down from the cab bed unaided, but Chigger didn't seem too pleased to see his rescuers. He did a lot of growling and snapping until I told him to knock it off. Then, ever hopeful of more mashed potatoes, he leapt from the back of the truck and followed me inside, as I trailed after the gurney Rob was on.

"Is he going to be all right?" I kept asking all the people who were working on him. But they wouldn't say. They were too busy barking off his vital signs and writing them down on charts. The weirdest part was when they unwrapped him, and I saw what the yellow thing that had been around him the whole time was.

Oh, just the "Don't Tread On Me" flag from the True Americans' meeting house.

The one with the giant hole in it, from where I'd accidentally blasted it with a shotgun.

It was as I was standing there staring at this that I heard a voice call my name. I looked around, and saw that Dr. Krantz, who was being worked on over on the next gurney, had regained consciousness. He gestured for me to come close. I edged in between all the doctors and nurses who were hovering around him and leaned down so that he could whisper to me.

"Jessica," he hissed. "Are you all right?"

"Oh, sure," I said, surprised. "I'm fine."

"And Mr. Wilkins?"

"I don't know," I said, throwing a glance over my shoulder. I couldn't see Rob, for all the doctors and nurses crowded around him. "I think he's going to be okay."

"And Seth?"

"He's fine," I said. "Really, Dr. Krantz, we're okay. You just concentrate on getting better, okay?"

But Dr. Krantz wasn't through. He had something else to say to me, something that seemed of vital importance for him to get off his chest. He reached out and grabbed the front of my coat, and pulled me closer.

"Jessica," he rasped, close to my ear.

I had a feeling I knew what he was going to say, so I tried to head him off at the pass.

"Dr. Krantz," I said. "Don't worry about thanking me. Really, it's all right. I'd have done the same for anybody. I was happy to do it."

But Dr. Krantz still wouldn't let me go. If anything, his grip on the front of my coat tightened.

"Jessica," he breathed, again. I leaned even closer, since he seemed to be having trouble making himself heard.

"Yes, Dr. Krantz?" I said.

"You," he rasped, "are the worst driver I have ever seen."

CHAPTER

18

The county hospital saw a lot of action that night. And that's not even counting having a pickup ram through its ambulance-bay doors.

It also admitted forty-eight new patients, seven of them in critical condition. Fortunately none of the people listed as critical were friends of mine. No, it looked as if most of the damage that was done that night was done to the True Americans. As I sat in the waiting room—they wouldn't let me in to see Rob once he'd been admitted, because I wasn't family—I saw each person as they were wheeled in.

Of course, that didn't start happening for a while, because it took a pretty long time for the fire engines and ambulances and police to get out to Jim Henderson's place. In fact, merely my explanation of *how* to get out there took a while. The police interviewed me for about forty minutes before the first squad car even started off in the direction of the True Americans' compound.

And I'm not too sure they believed what I told them. That might be one of the reasons they didn't go tearing off right away. I mean, a militia group, under attack by a ragtag band of bikers and truck drivers? Fortunately at some point, Dr. Krantz regained consciousness, and they were able to go in and confirm everything I'd said. He must have been pretty persuasive, too, because when I saw the sheriff leaving the examination room Dr. Krantz had been shoved into while the hospital staff scrambled to find a surgeon skilled enough to sew his leg back together, he looked pretty grim.

For a short while, the only person in the emergency waiting room with me was Seth. Well, Seth and Chigger. The hospital people weren't too happy about having a dog in their waiting room, but when I explained that I couldn't leave Chigger outside in the truck, as he would freeze, seeing as how the truck had no heat—nor much of a windshield left—they relented. And really, once I'd gotten him a few packs of peanut-butter Ritz crackers from the snack machine, Chigger was fine. He curled up on two of the plastic chairs and went right to sleep, worn out from his long ride and all that barking.

Seth's reunion with his parents, which came about ten minutes after our arrival, was touching in the extreme. The Blumenthals wept with happiness over seeing their son alive and in one

piece. When they heard about my part in bringing Seth home, they pulled me into their group
hug, which was fun, even though I assured them
that I had, in fact, played only a very small role in
the liberation of their son from the militia group
that had kidnaped him.

But when Seth, while explaining precisely
what the True Americans were all about, showed
his parents the burn on his hand, which I had sort
of forgotten about, they freaked out, and Seth got
whisked off to the burn unit to have the wound
treated.

So then it was just Chigger and me in the waiting room.

Finally, though, my parents, along with
Douglas and Mike and Claire (because the two of
them are attached at the hip) showed up, and we
had our own tearful reunion. Well, at least, my
mom cried. No one else did, really. And my mom
only cried because she was so relieved that Great-
aunt Rose had been wrong: Apparently the
whole time I'd been gone, she'd been telling
everyone that I had probably run off to Vegas to
find work as a blackjack dealer. She had seen a
show about teenage runaway blackjack dealers
on *Oprah*.

Great-aunt Rose, my dad said, was leaving on
the first bus out of town in the morning, whether
or not she was ready to go.

It was a little while after this that Mrs. Wilkins
showed up. I had called her right after I called
my parents. But Mrs. Wilkins, being family, was

let into the room where they were keeping Rob, so it wasn't like we had a chance to visit or anything. She only came out once, and that was to tell me that the doctor had said Rob was going to be all right. He had a concussion, but the doctor didn't think he'd have to stay in the hospital for more than a day or two, so long as he regained consciousness by morning. My dad told Mrs. Wilkins not to worry about her shifts at the restaurant while Rob was convalescing, so that was all right.

One thing my dad didn't ask—no one in my family did—was what Rob and I had been doing, saving Seth Blumenthal and battling the True Americans together. Mike and Claire and Douglas already knew, of course, but it didn't seem to occur to my parents to ask. Thank God.

All they wanted to know was was I all right, and would I come home now.

I said I was fine. Only I couldn't come home. Not, I told them, until I'd heard that Dr. Krantz was safely out of surgery.

If they thought this was weird, they didn't say so. They just nodded and went to get coffee from the machine over by the cafeteria, which, this late at night, was unfortunately closed. I was famished on account of having had nothing to eat since lunch, so we raided the snack machines some more. I had a pretty good dinner of Hostess apple pie and Fritos, some of which Chigger helped me eat. Much to my surprise, no one in my family seemed really to like Chigger, who was quite charming to all of them, sniffing each one carefully in case he or she had food hidden somewhere. My mom looked a little taken aback when I asked if I could keep Chigger. But she softened when I explained that the police had told me any pets found on seized property would be impounded and probably put down.

Besides, no one could deny Chigger made a very good guard dog. Even the cops had given him a pretty wide berth while they were questioning me.

And then, just as I'd suspected, about an hour after this, the first of the casualties from the battle of the Grits versus the True Americans began to flood the ER. I'm not sure, but I think it was around then that my parents began to suspect that my real motivation for staying at the hospital wasn't to find out whether or not Dr. Krantz's surgery had been successful. No, it was because I wanted to be there when they brought in Jim Henderson. I wanted to be there really, really bad.

Not because I had anything to say to him. What can one say to someone like him? He is never going to realize that we were right and he was wrong. People like Jim Henderson are incapable of changing their ways. They are going to believe in their half-assed opinions until the day they die, and nothing and no one is ever going to convince them that those beliefs might be mistaken.

No, I wanted to see Jim Henderson because I wanted to make sure they'd gotten him. That's all. I wanted to make sure that guy didn't slip away, didn't run off deeper into the hills to live in a cave, or escape to Canada. I wanted that guy in prison, where he belonged.

Or dead. Dead wouldn't have been too bad, either. Although I didn't think Jim Henderson could really ever be dead enough for me. At least in prison, I'd know he was suffering. Death seemed like too good a punishment for the likes of him.

And I wouldn't have been too sad to see Mrs. Henderson there in the morgue with him.

But though they brought in plenty of people I recognized as True Americans—all men, including the two from the four by four that had been chasing us, and Red Plaid Jacket, suffering from a bullet wound to the thigh—none of them were Jim Henderson. This was pretty disappointing, but certainly not unexpected. Of course a guy like him would run at the first sign of trouble. He wouldn't get far, though. Not with me on the case. I would make it my personal psychic business to know where he was and what he was doing at all times. That way I could alert the authorities, who would hopefully catch him when he least expected it. Like when he was sleeping, or maybe making more baby True Americans. Some time when he wasn't likely to be able to reach for a gun.

It was as I was examining the faces of the people being wheeled in, searching for Jim Henderson, that I saw one that looked more than a little familiar. I was up and out of my plastic seat in no time, and hurrying to the side of the gurney he was being wheeled in on.

"Chick," I cried, reaching for his arm, which had already been attached to an IV bottle. "Are you okay? What happened?"

Chick smiled wanly up at me.

"Hey, there, little lady," he said. "Glad to see you made it. Wilkins and the kid all right? How about the professor?"

"They're all fine," I said. "Or going to be fine, anyway. But what about you? What happened?"

"Aw." Chick looked irritably at the nurse who was trying to get a thermometer into his mouth. "Stun grenade went off early." He lifted his hands. I gasped at how raw and bloody they were.

"Chick!" I cried. "I'm so sorry!"

"Ah," he said, sheepishly. "It was my fault. I shoulda just thrown the stupid thing. But then I saw the guy had got all the women and children lined up in front of him, and I hesitated—"

"Jim Henderson, you mean?"

"Yeah," Chick said. "Bastard was using his wives and kids as the old human shield."

"Wait." I stared down at him. "*Wives?*"

"Well, sure," Chick said. "Guy like Jim Henderson's gonna keep God's chosen race going, he can't afford to be monogamous. Lady," he said, to the nurse with the thermometer, "I ain't got no fever. What I got is burnt-up hands."

The nurse glared at both Chick and me.

"No visitors," she said, pointing imperiously

at the plastic chairs, "in the ER. Get back to your seat. And keep that dog out of the trash cans!"

I looked and saw that Chigger had his head buried in the ambulance-bay trash can.

"But what about him?" I asked Chick, as the nurse, disgusted with me, began physically to push me from the crowded ER. "Jim Henderson? Did they catch him?"

"Don't know, honey," Chick called. "Place was a zoo by the time they got me out of there, cops and firemen and what all—"

"And stay out," the nurse said, as she closed the ER doors firmly on me.

I walked disconsolately over to Chigger and pulled on his leather studded collar, eventually managing to drag him away from the garbage . . . though I had to pull his nose out of a Dorito bag. "Bad dog," I said, mostly for my parents' benefit, so they could see what an excellent and responsible pet owner I was going to make.

It was as I was doing this that I heard my name called softly from behind me. I turned around, and there was Dr. Thompkins, in a blood-smeared operating gown.

"Oh," I said, holding onto Chigger's collar. The smell of the blood was making him mental. I swear, it was enough to make me think the True Americans never fed their dogs. "Hey."

My parents, seeing their neighbor from across the street, got up and came over, as well.

"I just operated," Dr. Thompkins said to me, "on the leg of a man who told me he had you to thank for keeping him from bleeding to death."

"Oh," I said, brightening. "Dr. Krantz. Is he all right?"

"He's fine," Dr. Thompkins said. "I was able to save the leg. That was certainly one of the more . . . *interesting* tourniquets I've seen applied."

"Yeah," I said, humbly. "Well, I did get an A. In sixth grade first aid."

"Yes," Dr. Thompkins said. "I imagine you did. Well, in any case, Dr. Krantz is going to be fine. He also explained to me how he happened to have been shot."

"Oh," I said, not certain where Tasha's dad was going with this part. Like if he was going to yell at me for being irresponsible or something. Had someone told him it was me who'd rammed a pickup through the ambulance bay doors? I wasn't sure. "Well," I said, lamely. "You know."

Dr. Thompkins did a surprising thing. He stuck his right hand out toward me.

"I'd like to thank you, Jessica," he said, "for your part in attempting to bring my son's killers to justice."

"Oh." I was a little shocked. Was that what I had done? I guess it was, sort of. Too bad I hadn't been able to catch the guy who'd been ultimately responsible. . . .

"No problem, Dr. Thompkins," I said, and slipped my hand into Nate's father's.

Just as I did so, yet another ambulance came wailing up to the doors I'd smashed. The doors to the back of the vehicle were flung open, and the paramedics wheeled out a man who had been severely injured. In fact, he was practically holding his intestines in place with one hand. He was still conscious, however. Conscious and looking all around him with wild, crazy, blue eyes.

"Dr. Thompkins," one of the paramedics cried. "This one's bad. BP a hundred over sixty, pulse—"

Jim Henderson. It was Jim Henderson on that gurney, with his guts hanging out.

So they'd got him. They'd got him after all.

"All right," Dr. Thompkins said, looking over the chart the paramedics handed to him. "Let's get him upstairs to surgery. Now."

A pair of ER nurses took over from the paramedics, and began wheeling Jim Henderson down the hall, toward the elevator. Dr. Thompkins followed them, and I followed Dr. Thompkins. Chigger followed me.

"Hey, Mr. Henderson," I said, when the nurses pulled the gurney to a halt outside the elevator doors.

Jim Henderson turned his head to look at me. For once, his crazy-eyed gaze focused enough to recognize me. I know he did, because I saw fear . . . yes, fear . . . in those otherwise vacant orbs of blue.

"Get that dog," one of the nurses said, "away from here. He'll infect the patient."

"Jessica," Dr. Thompkins said. The elevator doors opened. "I'll finish talking to you later. But right now, I have to operate on this man."

"You hear that, Mr. Henderson?" I asked the man on the gurney. "Dr. Thompkins here is going to operate on you. Do you know who Dr. Thompkins is, Mr. Henderson?"

Henderson couldn't reply because he had an oxygen mask over his mouth. But that was okay. I didn't need an answer from him anyway.

"Dr. Thompkins," I said, "is the father of that boy you left dead in that cornfield."

Dr. Thompkins, with a startled look down at his patient, took an involuntary step backward.

"Yes," I said to Dr. Thompkins. "That's right. This is the man who killed your son. Or at least ordered someone else to do it."

Dr. Thompkins stared down at Jim Henderson, who, it had to be admitted, looked pretty pathetic, with his guts out all over the place like that.

"I can't operate on this man," Dr. Thompkins said, his horror-stricken gaze never leaving the man on the gurney.

"Dr. Thompkins?" One of the nurses slipped into the elevator and lifted a phone from a panel in there. "You want me to page Dr. Levine?"

"Not to mention," I said, "this guy's also the one who kidnapped Seth Blumenthal, burned down the synagogue, and knocked over all the headstones in the Jewish cemetery."

The nurse hesitated. Dr. Thompkins continued to stare down at Jim Henderson, disgust mingling with disbelief on his face.

"How about Dr. Takahashi?" the other ER nurse suggested. "Isn't he on duty tonight?"

"Hmmm," I said. "Mr. Henderson doesn't like immigrants very much either. Right, Mr. Henderson?" I bent down so that my face was very close to his. "Gosh, this must be very upsetting to you. Either a black guy, a Jewish guy, or an immigrant is going to end up operating on you. Better hope all those things you've been saying about them are wrong. Well, okay, buh-bye, now."

I waved as the two nurses, along with a dazed Dr. Thompkins, stepped onto the elevator with Jim Henderson. The last thing I saw of him, he was staring at me with those wide, crazy eyes. I can't be sure, but I really do think he was reevaluating his whole belief system.

CHAPTER

19

Jim Henderson didn't die. Not on the operating table, anyway.

Drs. Levine and Takahashi operated on him, in the end. Dr. Thompkins excused himself. Which was pretty noble of him, actually. I mean, if it had been me, I don't know. I think I would have gone ahead. And let the scalpel slip at a crucial moment.

But Jim Henderson lived through his surgery. He owed his life to two people who came from religious and ethnic groups he'd been teaching his followers to hate. I kind of wondered how he felt about that, but not enough actually to ask him. I had way more important things to worry about.

Primarily, Rob.

It wasn't until the next day that Rob finally woke up. I was sitting right there when he did it.

I did go home right after the thing with Jim Henderson—actually, hospital security came along and threw me out, which is a terrible way, if you think about it, to treat a hero. But one of the ER nurses who'd escorted Jim Henderson to surgery apparently finked me out, saying I'd "threatened" a patient.

Which of course I had. But if you ask me, he fully deserved it.

Anyway, I went home with my parents and brothers and Claire, and got a few hours of sleep. I showered and changed and ate and walked Chigger and went a few rounds with my parents over him. They were not too thrilled to have a trained attack dog living under our roof, but after I explained to them that the cops would have sent him to the pound, and that the True Americans were not the world's best pet owners, as far as I can see, they came around. They weren't exactly thrilled with the way Chigger had chewed through an antique rug while we'd all been asleep, but after three or four bowls of Dog Chow, he was fine, so I don't see what the problem is. He was just *hungry*.

It hadn't been much of a surprise to me that on top of everything else, Jim Henderson and his followers turned out to be lousy pet owners.

Anyway, I was sitting there flipping through a copy of the local paper, which mentioned nothing about me and the important role I'd played in the capture of the dangerous and deranged leader of the largest militia group in the southern half of the state, when Rob started to come round. I put the paper down and ran for his mom, who'd also been waiting for him to wake up. She'd been down the hall getting coffee when he finally opened his eyes. She and I both hurried back to his room. . . .

But at the door, a voice from across the hall called weakly to me. When I turned, I saw Dr. Krantz lying in the bed of the room across from Rob's. Gathered around his bed were a number of people I recognized, including Special Agents Smith and Johnson, who used to be assigned to my case. Until Dr. Krantz fired them from it, that is. It was good to see they could all let bygones be bygones and get along.

"Well, well, well," I said, strolling into the crowded room. "What's this? A debriefing?"

Dr. Krantz laughed. It was a startling sound. I wasn't used to hearing him laugh.

"Jessica," he said. "I'm glad to see you. There are a couple of people here I want you to meet."

And then Dr. Krantz, whose leg was in a long sling, with spikes coming out of a metal thing around the patched-up wound where I'd stuffed my rock, pointed to various people crowded into the small room, and made introductions. One of the people was his wife (she looked *exactly* like him, except that she had hair). Another was a little old lady called Mrs. Pierce, whose name suited her, since she had very piercing eyes, as blue as the baby bootie she was industriously knitting. The last was a kid about my age, a boy named Malcolm. And of course I already knew Special Agents Johnson and Smith.

"That was quite the invasion of the True Americans' Compound you launched, Jessica," Special Agent Johnson said.

"Thanks," I said, modestly.

"Jessica's always impressed us," Special Agent Smith said, "with her communication skills. She seems to have a real flair for rallying people to her cause . . . whatever cause that happens to be."

"I couldn't have done it," I said, humbly, "without the help of many, many Grits."

There was an awkward silence after this, probably on account of no one in the room knowing what a Grit was, except for me.

"You'll be happy to know," Dr. Krantz said, "that Seth is going to be fine. The burn should heal without leaving a scar."

"Cool," I said. I wondered what was happening in Rob's room. He and his mom had probably had a nice little reunion by now. When was my turn?

"And the police officer," Dr. Krantz went on, "who was shot should be fine. As should all of your, um, friends. Particularly Mr. Chicken."

"Chick," I corrected him. "But that's great, too."

There was another silence. Malcolm, who was sitting over on the windowsill, playing with a Gameboy, looked up from it briefly, and said, "Jeez, go on. Ask her, already."

Dr. Krantz cleared his throat uncomfortably.

Special Agents Johnson and Smith exchanged nervous glances.

"Ask me what?" I knew, though. I already knew.

"Jessica," Special Agent Smith said. "We all seem to have gotten off on the wrong foot with you. I know how you feel about coming to work for us, but I just want you to know, it won't be like it was with . . . well, the first time. Dr. Krantz has been doing groundbreaking work with . . . people like yourself. Why, Mrs. Pierce and Malcolm here are part of his team."

Mrs. Pierce smiled at me kindly above the baby bootie. "That's right, dear," she said.

"It just really seems to me," Special Agent Smith said, reaching up to fiddle with her pearl earring, "that you would enjoy the work, Jessica. Especially considering your feelings about Mr. Henderson. Those are the kind of people Dr. Krantz and his team are after, you know. People like Jim Henderson."

I glanced at Dr. Krantz. He looked a lot less intimidating in his hospital gown than he did in his usual garb, a suit and tie.

"It's true, Jessica," he said. "Someone with powers like yours could really be a boon to our team. And we wouldn't require anything from you but a few hours a week of your time."

I eyed him warily. "Really? I wouldn't have to go live in Washington, or anything?"

"Not at all," Dr. Krantz said.

"And I could keep going to school?"

"Of course," Dr. Krantz said.

"And you'd keep it out of the press?" I asked. "I mean, you'd make sure it was a secret?"

"Jessica," Dr. Krantz said. "You saved my life. I owe you that much, at least."

I looked at Malcolm. He was absorbed in his video game, but as if he sensed my gaze on him, he looked up.

"You work for him?" I asked, gruffly. "You like it?"

Malcolm shrugged. "'s okay," he said. Then he turned back to his game. But I could tell by the way color was spreading over his cheeks that working for Dr. Krantz was more than just okay. It was a chance for this otherwise average-looking kid to make a difference. He'd wanted to seem cool about it in front of the others, but you could totally tell: This kid was way psyched about his job.

"How about you?" I asked Mrs. Pierce.

"Oh, my dear," the old lady said, with a beatific smile. "Helping to put away scumbags like that jerk Henderson is what I live for."

After this surprising remark, she turned back to the baby bootie.

Well.

I looked at Dr. Krantz. "Tell you what," I said. "I'll think about it, okay?"

"Fine," Dr. Krantz said, with a smile. "You do that."

I told him I hoped he felt better soon, said good-bye to the others, and drifted back across the hall.

So? Stranger things have happened than me joining an elite team of psychic crime-fighters, you know.

And it *had* felt pretty good when I'd seen them wheeling Jim Henderson in on that gurney. . . .

Inside Rob's room, Mrs. Wilkins had been joined by her brothers and Just-Call-Me-Gary.

"Oh," Rob's mom said, as I came in. "Here she is!"

Rob, his hair looking very dark against the whiteness of the bandage around his head, and the pillows behind his back, smiled at me wanly. It was the most beautiful smile I had ever seen. Instantly, all thoughts of Dr. Krantz and the Federal Bureau of Investigation left my head.

"Hi," I said, moving toward the bed. I had, for the occasion, donned a skirt. It was no velvet evening gown, but judging by the appreciative way his gray-eyed gaze roved over me, he sure thought it was.

"Well," Rob's uncle said. "What say we check out this cafeteria I've heard so much about, eh, Mary?"

Mrs. Wilkins said, "Oh, yes, let's." Then she and her brothers and Just-Call-Me-Gary left the room.

Hey, it wasn't subtle. But it worked. Rob and I were alone. Finally.

It was a little while later that I lifted my head from his shoulder, where I'd been resting it after having become exhausted from so much passionate kissing, and said, "Rob, I have to tell you something."

"I didn't ask you," he said, "because I didn't want you getting in trouble with your parents."

I looked at him like he was nuts. For a minute, I thought maybe he was. You know, that Mrs. Henderson had scrambled his brains with that mashed-potato bowl. "What are you talking about?"

"Randy's wedding," Rob said. "It's on Christmas Eve. No way your parents are going to let you go out on Christmas Eve. So you'd just have ended up lying to them, and getting in trouble, and I don't want that."

I blinked a few times. So *that* was why he hadn't asked me? Because he'd thought my parents wouldn't have let me go in the first place?

Happiness washed over me. But still, he could have just said so, rather than let me think he had some other girl in mind he wanted to take instead. . . .

I didn't let my relief show, however.

"Rob," I said. "Get over yourself. That's not what I was going to say."

He looked surprised. "It wasn't? Then what?"

I shook my head. "Besides," I said. "My parents would so totally let me go out on Christmas Eve. We don't do anything on Christmas Eve. It's Christmas Day that we do church and present opening and a big meal and everything."

"Fine," Rob said. "But don't tell me that you'd tell them the truth. About being with me, I mean. Admit it, Mastriani. You're ashamed of me. Because I'm a Grit."

"That is *not* true," I said. "*You're* the one who's ashamed of me! Because I'm a Townie. And still in high school."

"I will admit," Rob said, "that the fact that you're still in high school kind of sucks. I mean, it *is* a little weird for a guy my age to be going out with a sixteen-year-old."

I looked down at him disgustedly. "You're only two years older than me, nimrod."

"Whatever," Rob said. "Look. Do we have to talk about this now? Because in case you didn't notice, I've suffered a head injury, and calling me a nimrod is not making me feel any better."

"Well," I said, chewing on my lower lip. "What I'm about to say probably isn't going to make you feel better."

"What?" Rob said, looking wary.

"Your dad." I figured it was better if I just blurted it all out. "I saw a picture of him in your mom's room, and I know where he is."

Rob regarded me calmly. He did not even drop his hands from my arms, which he'd reached up to massage.

"Oh," was all he said.

"I didn't mean to pry," I said, quickly. "Really. I mean, I totally didn't do it on purpose. It's just, like I said, I saw his picture, and that night I dreamed about where he is. And I will totally tell you, if you want to know. But if you don't, that's fine, too, I will never say another word about it."

"Mastriani," Rob said, with a chuckle. "I know where he is."

My mouth dropped open. "You *know?* You *know* where he is?"

"Doing ten to twenty at the Oklahoma Men's State Penitentiary for armed robbery," Rob said. "Real swell guy, huh? And I'm just a chip off the old block. I bet you're real eager to introduce me to your parents now."

"But that's not what you're on probation for," I said, quickly. "I mean, something like armed robbery. You don't get probation for stuff like that, they lock you up. So whatever you did—"

"Whatever I did," Rob said, "was a mistake and isn't going to happen again."

But to my dismay, he let go of me, and put his hands behind his head. He wasn't chuckling anymore either.

"Rob," I said. "You don't think I care, do you? I mean, about your dad? We can't help who are relatives are." I thought about Great-aunt Rose, who'd never committed armed robbery—at least so far as I knew. Still, if being unpleasant was a crime, she'd have been locked up long ago. "I mean, if I don't care that you were arrested once, why would I care about—"

"You should care," Rob said. "Okay, Mastriani? You *should* care. And you should be going out on Saturday nights to dances, like a normal girl, not sneaking into secret militia enclaves and risking your life to stop psychopathic killers. . . ."

"Yeah?" I said, starting to get pissed. "Well, guess what? I'm not a normal girl, am I? I'm about as far from normal as you can get, and you know what? I happen to *like* who I am. So if you don't, well, you can just—"

Rob took his hands out from behind his head and took hold of my arms again. "Mastriani," he said.

"I mean it, Rob," I said, trying to shake him off. "I mean it, if you don't like me, you can just go to—"

"Mastriani," he said, again. And this time, instead of letting go of me, he dragged me down until my face was just inches from his. "That's the problem. I like you too much."

He was proving just how much he liked me when the door to his room swung open, and a startled voice went, "Oh! Excuse *me!*"

We broke apart. I swung around to see my brother Douglas standing there looking very red in the face. Beside him stood, of all people, a very abashed Tasha Thompkins.

"Oh," I said, casually. "Hey, Douglas. Hey, Tasha."

"Hey," Rob said, sounding a bit weak.

"Hey," Tasha said. She looked like she would have liked to run from the room. But my brother put a hand on her slender shoulder. My brother, Douglas, touched a girl—and she seemed to regain her composure somewhat.

"Jess," she said. "I just . . . I came to apologize. For what I said the other night. My father told me what you did—you know, about catching the people who did . . . that . . . to my brother, and I just . . ."

"It's okay, Tasha," I said. "Believe me."

"Yeah," Rob said. "It was a pleasure. Well, except for the part where I got hit with a mixing bowl."

"Mashed potatoes," I said.

"Mashed-potato bowl, I mean," Rob said.

"Really," I said to Tasha, who looked faintly alarmed by our banter. "It's okay, Tasha. I hope we can be friends."

"We can," Tasha said, her eyes bright with tears. "At least, I hope we can."

I held out my arms, and she moved into them, hugging me tightly. It was only when she got close enough for me to whisper into her ear that I said, softly, "You break my brother's heart, I'll break your face, understand?"

Tasha tensed in my arms. Then she released me and straightened. She didn't look upset, though. She looked excited and happy.

"Oh," she said, sniffling a little, but still reaching for Douglas's hand. "I won't. Don't worry."

Douglas looked alarmed, but not because Tasha had taken his hand.

"You won't what?" he asked. He darted a suspicious look at me. "Jess. What'd you say to her?"

"Nothing," I said, innocently, and sat down on Rob's bed.

And then, from behind them, a familiar voice went, "Knock knock," and my mother came barreling in, with my dad, Michael, Claire, Ruth, and Skip trailing along behind her.

"Just stopped by to see if you wanted to grab a

bite over at the restaurant. . . ." My mom's voice died away as soon as she saw where I was sitting. Or rather, who I was sitting so closely beside.

"Mom," I said, with a smile, not getting up. "Dad. Glad you're here. I'd like you to meet my boyfriend, Rob."

Jenny Carroll

Born in Indiana, Jenny Carroll spent her childhood in pursuit of air conditioning - which she found in the public library where she spent most of her time. She has lived in California and France and currently resides in New York City with her husband and a one-eyed cat named Henrietta. Jenny Carroll is the author of the hugely popular Mediator series as well as the bestselling Princess Diaries. Visit Jenny at her website, www.jennycarroll.com

Read Jenny Carroll's

the mediator

series in Pocket Books

the mediator

Shadowland

JENNY CARROLL

A new school, annoying step-brothers and disastrous first dates – these are nothing in comparison to Susannah's other problems. The ghostly hunk sitting in her new bedroom and the psycho spirit haunting the locker room who's out for revenge on her ex-boyfriend – that's what Susannah calls real trouble . . .

ISBN 07434 30506